Advance Praise for *Black Star*:

"Maureen Medved masterfully explores her protag-
onists in all their spangled, fallible glory. *Black Star*
plunges the reader into frantic academic rivalry. Is it
paranoia or master manipulation? Every twist and
turn will lead you down Medved's darkly
compelling rabbit hole."
— EDEN ROBINSON, author of *Son of a Trickster*

"*Black Star* delivers an indelible shimmer in a
bittersweet novel that is funny and fast and paranoid.
Black Star has a real voice, tragic and transcendent,
hallucinatory and very real, a jinxed collision of
charm and pain and eros and
maybe even atonement."
— MARK JARMAN, author of *19 Knives* and *My White Planet*

BLACK STAR

A Novel

Maureen Medved

ANVIL PRESS / CANADA / 2018

Anvil Press Publishers Inc.
P.O. Box 3008, Main Post Office
Vancouver, B.C. V6B 3X5 CANADA
www.anvilpress.com

Library and Archives Canada Cataloguing in Publication

Medved, Maureen, author
Black star / Maureen Medved.

ISBN 978-1-77214-112-2 (softcover)

I. Title.

PS8576.E228B53 2018   C813'.54   C2018-901147-5

Printed and bound in Canada
Cover design by Rayola Graphic Design
Interior by HeimatHouse
Represented in Canada by Publishers Group Canada
Distributed by Raincoast Books

The publisher gratefully acknowledges the financial assistance of the Canada
Council for the Arts, the Canada Book Fund, and the Province of British Columbia
through the B.C. Arts Council and the Book Publishing Tax Credit.

"Only descent into the hell of self-knowledge prepares the way for godliness."
— Immanuel Kant, *The Metaphysics of Morals*

I

EVERYTHING WAS PERFECT until Helene LeBec infected our university. A lesion of carcinogenic proportions capable of rotting and destroying departments and even entire institutions of higher learning.

"That's the kind of hire who is a department killer," said Tanis, my best friend, my colleague in the philosophy department. We'd look around to make sure no one heard us use the words "kill her" in The Perk, the faculty cafeteria. Somebody might call security.

LeBec, the cunning adjunct, was a coalescence of digital perversions: anime upskirt, cybernetic porn star, and wide-eyed schoolgirl. An erotic unicorn.

"Hello, Del!" She pronounced my name by elongating certain letters while curling the ends of others in a way that made me want to hurt her.

Del!

For Delorosa.

An homage to a great aunt. And as hot as an instrument of torture.

Why not just call me the Iron Maiden.

Del. Not an inspiration for dreams. Wet, dry, or otherwise.

Whereas LeBec was hot. Rockstar hot or the girlfriend-of-a-rockstar hot. She was sexy, pretty, smart, and I hated her.

I had a strong impulse to punch her. While that would be satisfying, I knew there'd be consequences.

"Wait until after you get tenure," Tanis said, biting into the kind of white and brown creamy snack that always looks better than it tastes.

Something procedural was always interfering with my plans.

An object can only grow to a certain point before its matter no longer retains the tension of the original form.

I felt relieved every time I dwelled upon LeBec's inevitable self-destruction.

Leave behind no evidence, John McGilvery would have said.

I have excellent credentials. One of the top five students at Wilbur Smith, a Fulbright scholar, a PhD from one Ivy League college, a Folding Chair at another.

My specialty: Different perceptions of reality. Publications: *The Real and the Unreal,* my first book. Current research: The decision as catalyst for personal and professional devastation.

After my work with John McGilvery, my mentor, my research shifted dramatically, morphing into my current interest in the area of philosophical decision theory, but no matter how hard I tried to steer the horse, it kept bucking and veering back into moral philosophy. I'd been working on *The Catastrophic Decision* for over a decade. I had written eight hundred pages and made an art project out of reassuring my colleagues the book was done, then analyzing their reactions.

"Great," said Denke, our Chair. He lifted the end of his sentence like a tween, code for hostility. "Let's get this wrapped up before the committee meets, okay?"

The committee he was talking about was the one for tenure and promotion. Their blade quivered across my neck. Denke and I had been having the same conversation for six years. Since that time, I'd promised I was in the final editing stages and about to submit it to publishers.

Even though I'd worked on this manuscript every day, I couldn't get it right. The process had become an exercise in masochism, involving a work of abstraction I could neither make sense of nor complete. Even though most academics I knew were publishing their peer-reviewed papers, my university now had aspirations to become a major research institute (one of the top 100, they kept telling us as if repeating it would make it so)—even though few outside of the area had ever heard of it.

Whenever I introduced myself at conferences, there was always an awkward silence. I often had to repeat myself several times as if whomever I was talking to thought that maybe I was making up the name of my university. Like what moron would pay to fly halfway across the world to attend a conference on decision theory and pretend they worked at a fake university? With their aspirations for "achievement," my department made it clear when I was hired that my job and my tenure hinged on a book deal. I had not yet obtained one. But that wasn't the reason I was writing *The Catastrophic Decision*. Over the years, my obsession had grown borderline irrational. My colleagues acted as if they cared about what they did even though that spark that once excited them had long fizzled out. No longer motivated by ideas, they were publishing the same research on repeat, accumulating citations, an "outstanding" h-index, massive student loads, and research money. But I considered their work subpar. I didn't want to circle inside myself like those thought experiments that McGilvery massaged repeatedly like a bad foot. I truly believed I was creating new philosophy by making sense of the shape of my life, which I viewed as a long flat line dipping beyond the vibrating horizon into Nowheresville or maybe Shitsville or maybe even Fucktown, USA.

How had my life come to this? I kept returning to and trudging through those abstract mental roads, performing the same thought experiments I'd rejected after my tenure with McGilvery. And every day an unsettled feeling twitched inside me that wouldn't go away unless I worked on my book. And whenever I stopped, the feeling would return. "Just do it!" Denke said. I wouldn't be pressured. I was on the verge of something.

A story had circulated. A philosopher had received a six-figure advance from a publisher. If the genie was real, I wasn't going to pass up my chance to rub the bottle. For the past two years, whenever Denke and I had "the conversation," his eyes pressed into me. "What's the hold up?" His voice became punitive, like a nun with a stick.

"I'm missing just one bolt that could pull this whole thing together."

Time had corroded Denke's faith in me. He was no longer willing to indulge my fantasies. "No time for perfectionism. Let's just hammer this thing out."

After a while, I noticed that any mention of the word "book" in my presence made Denke and the rest of my colleagues cringe and exchange looks.

Time was running out. A stranger passed me in the Quad. Tilley hat. Shorty shorts. Knee-high socks. An expression of confused abstraction. Once the alpha predator of our eco-system, such people now looked insane. Stalked, felled, driven to near extinction through the process of anagenesis and the sudden appearance of a more advanced life form, a kind of superior progeny of those better adapted to survive and reproduce in this high tech, ruthlessly competitive biophysical environment.

At forty, I was no supermodel.

Not, as my mother delighted to remind me, small boned.

But I'd found my brand. Whipped that trope. The naughty librarian. Dyed my white hair black. Wore bold, white plastic frames. Cool, but not ridiculous.

Stout. No-nonsense. Preoccupied by research. Predisposed to irritability. Not at the top of the party list. Not rude, but direct. Aggravated by people: mainly colleagues and family. But dealt with them in a perfunctory manner, keeping my expression blunt. Clomped through the halls as a courtesy, alerting others to my presence, in case they were talking about me. Lumbered from my office in the Department of Philosophy to the lecture theatre in John Kenneth Hall, in the basement of an abandoned building, incubated with asbestos. Black mold. I suspected my colleagues were trying to kill me

"Overcrowding," said Kalli, our department secretary.

Kalli. Formerly Joan. Dumped by her boyfriend, Rick. Made up her name at a weekend retreat. Apparently, Kalli had more numerological gravitas.

"It's time for the big shift," she'd announced.

Joan. Now Kalli. Blonde hair sprayed in a contemporized beehive. Too tight clothes jangled with fake gold. Nail emojis. Saturated in perfume. Somebody finally submitted a complaint that she was an environmental hazard. So it made sense then that she couldn't recognize the hazard of John Kenneth Hall.

"It's a good space," said Kalli. "And nobody'll be breathing down your neck."

"It doesn't look like I'm going to be breathing soon, either."

I was not your typical academic, an egg coddled in a pot by anxious and neurotic parents. Over the years, I'd fed my life through the shredder. Repurposed all the little pieces to make the life I have now with rigorous discipline. I researched night after night. Taught myself to think. To write.

My record demonstrates I have cultivated the respect of my students and peers.

But that LeBec.

Smiling that smile.

"Hello, Dellll!"

She elongated the end of my name out high, round, deliberately tinked it out.

I was a bright light. A scholar of import. Excellent, shining credentials.

I could never be out of my depth.

Despite McGilvery's recommendations, his shamefully glowing recommendations, I paid my price in blood. Passed up. At Yale. Harvard. Even at Northwestern. And ended up here, in the academic world of this small town university, where I have complete control and discipline over the mind. The untrained mind is useless in determining the difference between the real and the unreal.

HELENE LEBEC WAS an adjunct. A seasonal worker, cheaply paid. Trucked in for her expertise. Then sent back to wherever she came from.

In LeBec's case, some tiny college in Idaho, home of the potato.

"God's country," she said.

"Hmm. You talk as if God exists, and forgot about the rest of us," I said.

She stared back at me. Blinked as pure and sincere as a dog.

I first met Helene LeBec at our summer faculty meeting. Her outfit was audacious, even by the standards of our student population. That day she wore thigh-high boots. Her skirt so short it was probably a belt. Her giant anime eyes ticked open, that factory-inserted look known as Doll's Head. Her hair shattered shards of blue glass. The grommets and piercings.

A rudimentary life form nobody would want as a full faculty member. No student as a mentor.

Not everyone can be stellar. I felt sorry for her. The one with no future.

Initially, I thought LeBec was somebody's kid, coming for a "visit-your-parents-at-work-day." An undergraduate invited to our faculty meeting to make a brief announcement about a student initiative. The only podium I could imagine her standing on was the one at the Fuzzy Banana strip bar on Highway Number 5.

That day, Denke had that grating, crack-bender smile. I'd seen it before. LeBec was the consequence of some backroom negotiation. Some dirty exchange of funds. It was just a matter of time before Denke saw himself reflected in a pool of his own vomit then sent LeBec back to the potato farm.

My colleague, Blegg, was a logician. A bland face, cauliflower head sproinging with tight white curls. "I'm sorry, I'm pregnant," parenthetical to every statement.

I can't stand people who make excuses for their poor life choices.

That day at the faculty meeting, Blegg leaned over to me. Her blank eyes gave off a messianic flash under the fluorescent lights.

She always turned up with some bit of intrigue or gossip like someone who needed to fuck strangers to keep the marriage interesting. That day she keened into my ear the name of the Ivy League college where LeBec had received her PhD.

"What are you, her agent?" I said. "Don't try to sell me on her."

Once an adjunct myself, I was currently the youngest member of permanent faculty, hired for a tenure track position in philosophy of mind, based strictly on a rigourous interview process, letters of reference, the success of my first book, and the promise of a second.

When *The Real and the Unreal* came out ten years ago, it had a respectable following. LeBec stared at me throughout the meeting, vibrating with the wet frenzied wonder of an adolescent girl who'd met her teen crush.

As soon as Denke ended the meeting, and right in front of everyone, LeBec called out, "Del Hanks, I'm a fan!" I was taken aback. Nobody had ever admired and acknowledged my work so effusively in public.

My colleagues waited to gauge my response, smiling in that dark way I associated with predatory rapacity.

What I then said had to be perfect. Otherwise I'd be criticized, loathed, and shunned. I carved it out carefully. "Really? That's nice."

LeBec was a virtue ethicist with research on something to do with pets. Her PhD was a high contrast to her cute baby voice and intentionally choreographed slutty/hipster attire. It created a chemical reaction within me that instantly turned me into a bitch.

"Del, I love your work. Of course, when one considers your feminist perspective—"

I bristled. "There is remotely no feminist perspective in my work." Even I could taste the tartness of my own enunciation. It felt powerful to be hard and withholding toward LeBec, and I hated that aspect of myself. It made me feel bad, but not bad enough, I thought, as I smiled at my colleagues. "But you would know that since you love my work," I said with an emphasis on love. My colleagues shrunk in my cut.

The night after our faculty meeting, I had a nightmare. It

had the impact of an H-bomb dream, or the one about the asteroid hurtling toward the earth.

In this nightmare, an unknown postdoc received a six-figure advance from a major publisher. LeBec's face flashed whitely inside me. The saying, "It's only a dream," was quickly replaced by "No, it's fucking real!" Months earlier, Blegg had given me the grim details. I'd forgotten the writer's name until that night. I didn't want to confirm online. If true, I'd never sleep again.

I asked Tanis about it the next day.

"That's the one. I thought you knew that." She said it like a slap.

The words "No fucking way!" came out before I could filter them.

Tanis shrugged. "I don't think fucking had anything to do with it."

It seemed hard to believe that the writer with the big advance was the same person who looked like a sullen teenager painting her toenails in the sun.

Although I'm sure it wasn't the first time, I had literally never heard of such a big advance for an academic publication. A hive of envy and rage swarmed inside me.

It was LeBec! Not even a famous person. Not even a regular person. Not someone who'd paid their dues after decades of research, like Tanis or that idiot Denke.

After that, it was all the LeBec show. All the time. How she'd accepted and rejected invitations. Flew all over the world. A phenomenon. Genetically superior. Some ultra species created in a lab.

For that kind of money, I'd join a circle jerk with Kant, Plato, and Spinoza.

"How do you get that kind of advance?" I asked Tanis.

"You're not that kind of philosopher," Tanis said. "Forget it."

Her comment cut my heart. Then my heart sagged at the tight margins of my destiny. I couldn't tolerate the pain of what she'd said and still maintain our friendship. I angled her comment for days until it caught a piece of light. I decided she must have meant that I was too principled to exploit the lurid and macabre for fame and money.

I was soon coming up for review before the Senior Tenure and Promotions Committee. One month after the faculty meeting, and one week before the start of the fall term, Denke had summoned me to his office.

Brian Denke had built his reputation on five small books on Descartes, and had been repeatedly appointed Chair based on a full-spectrum diplomacy that was about as compelling as a tube of Polysporin. He lacked imagination, but didn't alienate people either. Fiftyish, medium height and build. He wore beige chinos and plaid button-down shirts, and had a mole that distinguished him from the rest of my colleagues.

"Your CV is in good shape. The reference letters are forthcoming."

The mention of those letters made the tight ball inside me clench and turn. No one could find out what I had to do to get them.

"Should I have confidence in my promotion?"

He nodded. Then advised I submit for early tenure.

"I thought I had another year."

"Strike when the iron's hot," he said.

Was it hot? More like a fork I'd stuck in a cake and forgotten in the refrigerator. The idea terrified me. I made decisions with careful, measured deliberation. But fearing they might view my hesitation with disfavour, I agreed to the early promotion. A sickle of foreboding and shame hooked inside me.

That night, I climbed the Lin Tower, looking out onto the university quadrangle to the forest beyond. The tiny iron filings clustered at the edges. The students. The dying sun squeezed between the holes of leaves. The ink that saturates this world.

I needed my life to beat and tick to the end of my tenure clock.

Best to have a perfect file. A slam dunk, as Denke called it.

While I have excellent credentials, my file was far from perfect. Then I castigated myself for not waiting another year. I had one book. I should have waited for a second book before agreeing to Denke's plan.

Changing my mind would be a sign of instability and weakness.

If I did not get tenure, I would not humiliate myself through the appeal process.

I hadn't prepared for such an outcome. I would never recover. I would probably have to kill myself. At forty, I couldn't do anything else.

I considered the options: telemarketer, phone-sex operator, or death—something requiring no physical presence, but with the whiff, or suggestion, of cunt.

Over the past almost twenty years I had climbed carefully along this twisted bridge. I now suspected that my application for early promotion and tenure was ill-advised, arriving before the seven-year termination of my tenure clock. As Denke was Chair, I had no reason to question his recommendation. But with the sudden arrival of LeBec, it crossed my mind that maybe the committee wouldn't approve my tenure. Only one flexible F-Slot existed. My F-slot. A faculty slot. The currency in which the value of each of us is weighted. These thoughts were irrational and even paranoid; Denke and the others had invested too much in my being here.

The next day, I made my way to my first class of the term at John Kenneth Hall. It was in the basement of an abandoned ten-storey building that was connected to the philosophy department by a tunnel. I noticed that stairwell as I passed it. A pair of eyes shivered out from the space beneath it.

Students and faculty crossed in both directions to get to Philosophy and the other humanities, often cutting through this remote location. I then noticed a few of the students eyed the stairwell person as they passed. And even though some of them skimmed my eyes with theirs, questioning if what they had seen was real, I did not acknowledge this exchange and the existence of this person under the stairwell. I knew better than to get involved in anything controversial and gave them a blank stare. Discipline the mind. If you don't see it, maybe it isn't there.

"Look at you. Just look at you," my mother would've said.

Months after my father's death, my mother died of dementia. The grey lacunae devoured the meat of her brain, leaving a dry and fragile web.

And where was Clint? My brother never bobbled up from his dank well. He was like a Magic 8 Ball: Yes. No. Go Fuck Yourself—unless his wife forced him to leave the house or his dealer had stopped by with a delivery.

I was convinced that, like Clint, I was incapable of love. I had no real feeling toward my mother. Every time I'd go near her, a cold metallic repulsion would line the inside of my skin. I then assumed (who doesn't love their mother?) that I may have been somewhere on the spectrum, the one where you're lacking empathy and missing that integral frontal lobe. I could rarely even crack a laugh unless it was at someone else's expense. But most laughs were at my expense and that made me want to cry. I felt relieved whenever I thought that I finally had an explanation for how I was.

As my mother disintegrated, I held onto her wrist, careful not to apply too much pressure. Her personality frayed apart, then dissolved anyway. But it made her a nicer person, I thought, as she smiled at me, bewildered from her hospital bed.

"Can't we just keep her like this?" I asked the doctor.

The doctor: dour, but with a chipper little Dutch boy haircut, hadn't looked up as she clapped her file together. "Your mother will die in two months."

How protective I became of this creature who gave me life, but whose life I'd spent my own wanting to destroy. So I amazed even myself when I shot the doctor a look, and said, "That was a stupid thing to say in front of the patient."

We turned to my mother, who gleamed as if we'd handed her an ice-cream cone.

After that, I had called the hospital every week, exactly like a diligent daughter.

"Good if you could make it down," the doctor said.

"Is it time?"

I flew in twice to see my mother. Both times she sat exactly where I'd left her, with the same deranged expression pasted on her face. I turned to the doctor. "What's up?"

"She took a positive turn. I thought you'd be pleased."

"Don't cry wolf," I told the doctor. "I have a job."

With both of her children gone, my mother was alone and

couldn't remember why she had to eat. An urgency escalated inside me. Before I left, I'd made a poster that read EAT OR DIE and taped it to the wall as she gleamed at me from her hospital bed. Still, two months later, my mother shrank, then vanished on schedule.

I stepped out of my lecture to receive the call.

"We're sorry to inform you," the nurse had said. She held out that phrase like a diaper loaded with shit. What did she expect me to do with it?

Where was the doctor? Interesting how they disappear when you need them. Fear and sorrow choked me. "What did you do to her? She was fine two months ago."

"Things can change very fast," she said in a practiced way.

I wanted to cry. But I said, "That just sounds like an excuse."

After my mother died, rage still picked at me like a bad marriage. Underneath the rage, swelled sorrow. And underneath the sorrow, that metallic foil lined the inside of my skin. I didn't know what it was, and it terrified me.

Well, it was a year ago, but at least she was finally dead.

Thank God for miracles, I said, imitating my childhood Pastor, Kevin. Beige suits, monosyllabic gutturals, Jesus, the rapture, blathering on about worse than nothing until I wanted to build and jump into my own fiery pit.

And while I thought I'd never have to see her again, my mother resurfaced from the grave to torture me, just as she always had ever since my metamorphosis.

I'd torn myself away from that choked chrysalis of Slaughter—known as Manslaughter—Street. Night changed the dirty white streets into something dark and oily. Our grey flat hovered above that store of Slaughter. The neighbourhood crumbled. Then collapsed. Shops boarded up more as more girls buckled on spiked heels. More gangs loitered on corners, streetlights flashing in their eyes and off their teeth.

Jesus is Lord and Union Gospel thrift stores. Pasteur Fried Chicken. Roosevelt and Hazel hotels. The Regent. Every day I walked home from my high school, Wilbur Smith. Books dangled and slapped my thighs like cow udders.

Philosophy wore through those dirty sheets of Slaughter. Tiny hopeful stars glinted then disappeared, depending on the light. I mistook this phenomenon for some sign or manifestation that led me to my fate. I didn't know then that what I thought I saw with my visual system was not real, but something scientists now know they can gauge by optical and neurological properties. But those tiny stars were probably the last thing I noticed on Slaughter as I used my mind to separate myself from that place with the precision of a surgeon's blade.

Night after night, I trudged through intricate volumes. Twisted veins of long, difficult discourse pulsed, then atrophied, under my fingers.

I studied with difficult discipline. Then on through those difficult, disciplined years beyond the streets of Slaughter, academic awards, Ivy League institutions. I attained degrees, a postdoc, and teaching positions that took me here.

Be careful what you wish for!

"Look at you. Just look at you. Buried in book after book, night after night, thinking you could ever really get away. Nice try!"

"Thanks for the vote of confidence, Mother."

No matter what my mother said, I still reached this position.

"Sad you have to settle for a place like that. Where is it again?"

Then about my bid for tenure, "Huh! I doubt they'll ever

buy your bid. You'll be back." She huffed a laugh. "You've made your bid. Now you'll have to lie in it."

I'd sequestered myself in academic solitude for more than twenty years.

No longer the short-term sessional, adjunct, or postdoc. My existence at whatever institution so fleeting that nobody wanted to invest in me.

I went to work, taught my classes, came home, ate in front of the TV, then worked on my manuscript. Aside from tenure, it was the only thing that mattered any more. I embraced them like a set of conjoined twins who were warped by their very interpenetration, but whom I could neither reject nor kill. The university was located in a town I'd never heard of before I'd applied for this job as Assistant Professor of Philosophy, tenure track.

It was too rainy. Too green. Too many trees.

I knew the mountains were there, but you couldn't see them. Even six years later, I didn't feel a part of the place.

Here where the ocean swallows the rainforest, the rainforest swallows the mountains, one dark mouth devouring another.

The black rain. Evergreen trees. Sharp triangles. Divide us from this world and every other. Buds clamped tight, discouraged from unfurling even a limb.

I'd climbed ranks. Made sacrifices. After those disciplined, grueling years. I'd accepted their offer. Settled here. Sucked into this place that glints so darkly.

Unlike the ambrosia salad, I am not a delightful addition to any festive occasion. I may come across as obdurate. Too direct. A bitch.

But I am painfully shy, especially around my colleagues.

No tiny cluster had called me over in our halls to gossip or solicit my opinion. Over the years, the clusters had tightened. And grown.

SINCE THE BEGINNING of the term, LeBec sought me out as if she wanted something in that needy, helpless way that reads as manipulative. Sometimes the evidence is palpable, yet too subtle to label. Her eyes groped mine. The tink of her voice picked inside me. Drew a tiny forced ball at the end of my name, Del.

She blocked me as I walked down the hall.

"Do you have time for a coffee, Del?"

"I wish!" I said. Made a throat-cutting action with my finger.

"Guess I caught you at a bad time."

"Tenure, you know." Nobody had time to "hang out." This wasn't grade eight.

I had a strong impulse to be cruel. But under that was a yearning. I wanted to hang out with someone, anyone. Even LeBec. But I was afraid that people would see us together, question my judgment, or think I was trying to home in on Denke's protégé.

Two days later, under the stairwell flashed a quick shift of light. My body fired off rapid signals of fear. His knees tucked under his chin. An orange sleeping bag next to him like a dog. Eyes studied me for some later degrading purpose.

I figured he was about twenty. Half my age! Sprung as tight as a jackknife, pale skin. Black shards of hair. Long dirty black coat, backward ball cap and hoodie. Based on the evidence, he smelled. More than the average citizen was equipped to handle. Government workers addressed the needs of the homeless.

I wanted to report him immediately.

But no time for a departure from your routine.

Tenure. Tenure. Keep your eye on the prize.

The linoleum rippled under the dim yellow lights. I strode to the classroom. Set up at the lectern. My students filed in with their skateboards. Knapsacks. iPads.

Now he's been found out. He'll be gone.

The next day he wasn't gone.

Even within a week, he was still there, staring at me from behind those sharp triangles of hair.

Do not be intimidated. Limit your association. You have a faculty position. Principles of conduct. Practices rigidly prescribed. The academic must maintain strict decorum. You are a public figure. No mental breakdowns or public nudity. This wasn't the seventies. Or even the eighties. Do not use the universal masculine pronoun. I didn't look to the stairwell once when I passed him. No other route to this remote lecture theatre. It would only be a matter of time before he became bored and went away. He was as inconsequential as the dust motes rotating above my head.

Then one day as I delivered my lecture, the room vibrated with tension. My gaze shifted to the door. His face was bending behind the beveled glass. I hardened until the deformed lush of colours and shapes trembled and broke. Even though I wouldn't look directly at him, from the sides of my eyes, I began to notice that he became alert whenever he saw me, eliciting permission to approach. I wouldn't grant it. Yet he was still there. No matter how tight I made the line of my mouth. No matter how hard my eyes.

I WAS FORTY. Had clear limits set by a mind grounded in reason.

Be realistic.

You know what you look like. Chop of dyed black hair. Weird white glasses. Not LeBec who leaned hard on her youth and beauty and could pass as a graduate student.

Time to shift to the world of the mind, I would repeat to myself like a cell phone notification. Over time my biology had reduced me.

My neck crooked over my laptop. I spent my days at the university and my nights propped up on my bed at home. Even though I had bought a queen, I worked and slept in the same tiny corner of my mattress. Ambitious going with the queen over a double I thought smugly. Against the walls of the warehouse, mattresses stacked up like bodies. According to Reddit, Matricide had excellent factory conditions.

The salesman wore his plaid shirt buttoned all the way to the neck, man bun, and Fathers-of-Confederation beard. His self-consciously stylized image antagonized me.

"Just give me something I don't have to flip and lasts thirty years. By then I should be ready for assisted living or dead. They provide the beds."

I bought the mattress six years ago. I still hadn't shared it with anyone. I was saving the rest of the bed for some special event that never arrived.

I told Tanis, "I'm amazed I don't have bed sores."

Around the time of the arrival of both LeBec and the stairwell man, my body, not unlike a serial killer, left behind a grotesque souvenir. One night something disengaged and gave way under my jaw.

I examined my face in the hand mirror I kept masochistically by my bedside. My jaw bunched into a fleshy wattle. I asked the ENT about it when I went to get my ear wax blown out. "It happens to aging women," he told me.

He didn't look at me. Scratched away in his file. Probably writing the standard letter to my GP: Thank you for referring this pleasant forty-year-old woman.

"You've got a prolapse."

"What? You mean like a vagina?"

The word vagina suddenly seemed hideous to me.

"You've got a large neck. You might consider losing some weight."

He asked me to stick out my tongue then wag it from side to side.

"Your tongue is too big for your mouth."

"I've never heard that complaint before."

The doctor grimaced. Scribbled on a pad. Tore off the page.

"Ask your dentist for a mouth guard."

"I'M GLAD I'M not playing the field," I told Tanis one night at the Garrote. We'd confessed our dirty secrets like girls at a slumber party.

"Now I finally get the appeal of assisted suicide. All I need is a helium balloon machine, a bottle of pills, a plastic bag, and I'm good."

"Come on, Del! Glass half full, remember?"

"Maybe I could take this on the road. Does the circus still have sideshows? Come see the woman with a prolapsed vagina on her neck."

I used my hand to demonstrate a talking-vagina neck.

"That's what online porn is for." Tanis tipped back her drink. Then hesitated. "I've had thoughts of cashing it in myself."

Her mouth didn't form its usual sardonic curl. Then her eyes turned into big circles like a little girl watching a scary movie.

"When you get a terminal diagnosis, shit gets real. You just want to grab death and say, okay Bitch, let's hug this one out."

"Did something happen?"

The anxiety strained through my voice like when I'd first registered the diagnosis of my mother's dementia.

Her eyes became distant, as if I'd caught her in a lie. Then she went very still and whispered, "Cancer."

She sucked in a bit of air and laughed as if she'd said something dirty and impulsive. The incongruity of it scared me.

I lowered my voice. "What are they going to do?"

She gave me a strange little smile. Looked down suddenly as if one of her intestines had fallen out, and she had to tuck it back in.

"I'm sorry I said anything. I'm actually okay."

"What do you mean okay?"

My adult years were now, officially, over. I was middle aged. It had gone too fast. Each phase smacked me in the face and ran away like a child playing a game.

Not a game. Real! Horrifyingly, bitterly, irrevocably real.

The stages. They came. Went. My life. Things I took for granted. Gone. I'd never get them back. Almost over. Middle age, too, soon would be over.

Even there at the Garrote, my muscles slackened. Skin slithered off the bone. Observe the common fruit. A peach, still a peach, even while rotting off the tree. Yet only the starving will eat it. And the birds who will eat anything.

Resist temptation.

Don't eat a piece of rotten fruit. Especially, when something ripe appears. You are what you eat, remember? Most prefer even the hard and green to the putrefying.

Why didn't anyone warn me?

I wanted to cry.

Where was my mother? Her mother? Who had this responsibility to teach us how to live? Oh, yes! It was the fashion magazines. This crucial role in raising young women had been abdicated to them and their glossy lies?

Sitting there with Tanis, I wanted to fix that feeling, but didn't have the skill set. Open a space, advises the Learning Education Aptitude Program (LEAP), our university's seminars for the reprobate academic.

Do not resist decrepitude! Shrink, slide, retract from the living. It's your time! Ripe, putrefying or other? I vacillated between ripe and other with an intermittent and terrifying bleat from putrefying, a nagging anxiety preparing one for the next stage. Nature's warning bell.

Where do you fit on a scale from one to ten?

If you don't know, it's time to re-brand.

MY BID FOR tenure squeezed its way through the decision makers. It grew so close I could almost touch it. I lingered at the door, scoping the hall for stragglers. Every day the person lodged under the stairwell, staring, a tiny perfect sarcophagus shrouded by medallions of light and dust. Still the long dirty coat, the hoodie pulled up over his cap as if he were waiting for me to snap. I would not acknowledge him and retreated to my classroom.

He posed a risk.

Proceed with caution!

Later, when my colleagues examine this account, I hope they will accept my version of events. Accuracy is key. Don't fabricate. Question the senses.

I am not a therapist or a worker for the city. Let someone else help him.

I should never even have looked.

Each day he glowed at the lecture hall door. An open disregard for the rules and the principles of conduct of our illustrious academic institution.

Our third-rate institution had aspirations to compete for the same public and private resources as second-rate institutions.

The second-raters competed with the first-raters and the Ivy Leaguers.

This pressure for achievement threatened to create a gravitational field so intense nothing could escape.

This stairwell person would not go away. Pushed me past my rational limits. Stepped out and out and out, staring at me hard as if I owed him some form of connection. He left me no choice. I would call someone. Security! The police!

I fondled my cell phone, who I often thought of as more than a friend.

Who was he? I could have walked away. I could have reported him.

Wanted to tell someone.

I had not one single ally left.

Never make a mistake.

Especially never tell that Helene LeBec. Only an adjunct lecturer. But a cunning adjunct. I suspected her as someone out to pluck me from my ledge, smiling that bright smile as if she was thinking something funny about me.

LeBec headed Academics for Social Change. Spoke seven languages. Had a book she'd managed to publish in twenty territories.

I didn't even know there were twenty territories.

Poor LeBec! we all thought. A lost cause.

Even Kalli sensed something about LeBec.

"She's watching you. It's kind of creepy."

For once I agreed with Kalli. LeBec was creepy. Her flattery and attention. Her ignorance of social proximity forced me to tilt back in her presence.

She'd arrived in July. Just two months earlier. Her smile charged with some insane, disordered hallucination. Mental illness, I postulated. Drugs. A tiny intelligence, pointed and alert, crackled under the surface of that smile. This was strategic.

She lavished me with praise. Make no mistake. And strictly do not engage with the obsequious. They have nothing but contempt for the focus of their attention.

"Dellll!" she said.

"Where are you from?" I asked her.

She stopped. A bird shot in midflight. "Idaho."

"I detect an accent."

"Really? That's funny."

"Idaho, isn't that where all the Nazis come from?"

I exchanged a knowing look with my colleagues as if we were in the presence of a child who'd stuck her hand in the cake. But no matter how cute, funny, and adorable, even children become tiresome.

LeBec looked bewildered. Then ruptured with an awkward, too-loud laugh.

Poor LeBec!

My colleagues smirked. You are so funny, Del. We never get tired of your witty whip-snappers. What would the academe be like without you?

Dull! Dull! Dull!

But of course I never got those endorsements. No much needed postmortem to dissect my personality.

One day when they ask me, I will tell them maybe I'd gone too far. My private thoughts terrified me. Charged in my head like wild horses with dark, pulsating flanks.

One day I will say something that will implicate me. I will risk my position.

But wait. Wait until tenure.

Timing is everything!

Just as I waited for the notification of her imminent departure.

It was still only September. She had to go. Close your eyes and hold your breath.

Three. Two. One.

Now caught between cancer treatments, Tanis looked bloated and groggy like someone arriving from a kegger.

"When is she leaving?" I whined as LeBec minced past us.

"Don't be pushy, Del!"

I CAUGHT BLEGG, Denke, Mahon and the others clustered around LeBec in the hall like a corsage when really they should have been working in their offices.

"I don't really know if Kant would agree that animals are irrational."

She fired off her opinions in the hall. Dangerous, like a

maniac with a gun. She didn't blink for an interminable length of time.

"What you just said makes no sense," I said.

Now I wish I could crawl back under those words.

LeBec looked away. Then turned her gaze back on me with a penetrative, almost threatening focus. "Del, is it true that you were once a Kantian?"

By the look on her face, that tiny smile as if she'd thought of a joke, LeBec knew exactly what she was doing, and was doing it to me with malevolent intention. I strongly suspected she had information about me, and it wasn't good. And although the others couldn't tell, I knew and she knew she was trying to undermine and hurt me.

I didn't say anything. I allowed an acceptable length of time to pass until my colleagues became reabsorbed by some inane circular discussion about whether Epicureanism could justify our need for reality TV. Then I walked away as hard and as fast as I could back to my office.

There was a backstory to this hideous narrative. Almost twenty years ago, I had received the single academic scholarship at Wilbur Smith, awarded to the highest ranked graduating student at my high school. The scholarship was a full-ride and paid for my tuition and my residence at Mary Seaman Hall for my entire undergraduate degree at a prestigious Ivy League institution. The university was in the same town as Slaughter, and I still crossed the tracks from the stone and statuary to the murderous and dilapidated to pitch in at the store sometimes. The scholarship was called the Davis Pierce, named after the person who crawled over the broken glass of Slaughter to this college and then used his connections to amass a fortune in the tobacco industry where he had held an executive position.

Apparently, he needed to do something to wipe the blood money off his hands. The name of the scholarship was later changed to the Wilbur Smith Cerebral Scholarship—which the students then morphed into the Cereal, and then the Serial Killer—but the Cerebral was still viewed as a more salubrious name to cut the link between child smokers and a high school scholarship. During that time at university, and long after, John McGilvery had written my letters of reference. And maybe even helped a little with my first book. I would not say he *wrote* my book. That would be inaccurate. But it would not be inaccurate to say he may have over-helped in the writing of my book. He was responsible for my position. All my positions. It would also be true to acknowledge that we may have had an understanding based on prior issues between us, and a kind of arrangement. Times have changed. The world is not even close to what it was in the eighties, or even the nineties. Rules of engagement that may have been marginally questioned then are now condemned and discussed in hushed whispers in tiny corners of our institution. If at all. Certainly, that's a good thing. Progress! This isn't the Paleolithic era. We can't go dragging people around by their hair. But now there's not even a cushion of tolerance for discussion and debate on matters that occurred in the past—even within an historical context. Yes, there are ambiguities and nuances that people do not want to address. Trying to make sense of this, and my part within it, has become one of my motivations for writing *The Catastrophic Decision*. But I didn't want people interfering in my business, especially now, during this pre-tenure time. This time of no tolerance. LeBec knew more than she let on about what brought me here. And so her brutal attack forced me to return to my manuscript again and again.

The Catastrophic Decision:
Perils of Moral Decision-Making

A sample of random notes from, *The Catastrophic Decision: Perils of Moral Decision-Making.*

Or,

Is a truly moral decision even possible?

Some, such as John McGilvery, question the concept of the truly moral decision.

McGilvery disproves all ethical positions, ultimately rejecting the idea that analytic philosophy can support ethical decision-making. He brings these points together and discounts them for a more phenomenological approach to ethics, dating back to Heraclitus.

I will argue that a truly moral decision can and must be attained through the rigours of an analytic process, and if people were equipped with such a process they could avoid catastrophic decisions. I will return to my thought experiments to find the correct way to parse these dilemmas in order to reach a true moral decision.

Even though we've tried and tried, and philosophers have continued to debate and publish on this topic since Socrates, we have achieved little traction on this issue.

What if a philosopher had all the information and tools for analysis required to make a morally sound decision and yet could still only make one that led to catastrophe?

Often after a tragedy, people will cry and lament, Why me?

(Note: Oedipus himself could certainly offer a seminar.)

How could I not have known the right thing to do in this situation?

I argue that sometimes, in some very extreme and complex cases, finding one's way to a truly moral decision is challenging.

Sometimes it's only through either accidentally making the right decision, or through a catastrophic result, that we can know a decision is truly moral.

EXAMPLE:

Let's turn to Last Meal. Say it's the night before your execution and you're offered the cake or the pie. You only get one choice and it's your final. You prefer cake, but as you know you will never have another dessert you want it to be a good one. How do you determine which is better, the cake or the pie? You ask the guard to describe both, but still the choice is unclear.

Here is one approach to this problem:

1. Consider the information, e.g., ask the chef for a list of ingredients.

Note 1: What is right and wrong? Is there a clear distinction?

Note 2: Always choose the most optimistic model [maybe the one who doesn't carry diuretics in her purse].

2. Weigh values against outcomes in the calculus of utility.

3. Parse potential outcomes. Choose outcomes with the highest value, e.g., cake always superior to pie.

4. What if the cake is low quality, too sweet, too dry? Return to potential outcomes.

5. Choose a more optimistic outcome, rinse, repeat.

6A. What if I don't like cake and I've never had it before and the cake, should I eat it, might taste really horrible, e.g., too sweet, too sour. Is there really such a thing as a cake nobody wants to eat? E.g., the one with the razor blades inside it or worse?

What's worse than razor blades?

Let's turn to moral considerations:

Maybe the cake will kill me, or cause me to kill someone else, e.g., laced with bath salts that will incite me to eat the face of another.

6B. But as I consider the needs of the other and myself, I can't make a decision because I don't know the relevant question to lead to a truly moral decision.

7A. If I want to eat cake, but cake means the death of another, what is important, my need to eat cake or the other's life? Do I eat the cake at the expense of the other?

7B. I must understand the interests of ourselves in relation to others. If I want to eat cake, but staying there leads to the death of another, then the decision is between my interests and the interests of the other.

Hence, who is important here: me or the other?

7c. Let's begin by dividing everyone into two categories: persons and others (others aren't rational: this would include most of my colleagues).

People say it's the first bump that gets them hooked. With the arrival of LeBec and my early tenure push, I was terrified to open my manuscript, but I began to gain momentum again. I might actually make it on Denke's schedule. I was on the verge, so close I could taste it. I began to believe that my initial assessment was right and that it was legitimate research. Maybe I could pull this off in time.

Yet as I hashed out my ideas, I considered the threats that surrounded me. LeBec was a threat; the stairwell person was a threat. This wasn't the eighties anymore. These were strange times. The Stalinists were watching from every corner, taking notes. Any involvement with the homeless could compromise my situation with the committee.

"You didn't see a guy living under the stairwell?"

"I was preoccupied," I'd tell them.

"Typical spaced-out academic," they'd say.

If being clueless was the worst crime they could accuse me of, I'd be fine. But in his own small way, he was trying to incriminate me. To suck me in.

With every pass, he'd step and angle toward me.

Anything I did would be a mistake. If I reported him, they'd say: How could you not be sensitive to the plight of the homeless and the marginalized?

I wanted to report him, but I felt like too much time had passed since I first saw him, and that would somehow get me into trouble. And although I knew it made no sense, I had a thought that maybe if I contributed to him being put out, my colleagues would see me as an insensitive complainer. Conversely, if he caused anyone harm that too could be a problem. The university encouraged what they called an environment of tolerance, which included helping the homeless, which they no longer called homeless (that's a lack, it's personal, too name-calling), and now called the hardest to house. In other words, if you didn't have a house, we weren't going to be assholes about it and shove it in your face. There was a man who sat in a dirty Santa hat with a yellow beard and undershirt yelling all year near the bus loop at our university. He was harmless. Still wearing a yellow beard and undershirt. Still at the bus loop. Still yelling. I didn't want to be the one to create a wall between us and them. The intolerant one. Especially with LeBec chairing Academics for Social Change.

If I didn't report him, they'd say: How could you not have known he was there and put us all at risk, especially the students! Now ten students are dead because of you. Stranger danger! Even a child knows. What's wrong with you?

Still, I continued to ignore the stairwell man. My best move would be to say I never saw him. If anyone were to ask about this ever: Deny! Deny! Deny!

Lie if necessary! John McGilvery would've said.

Nothing sweeter than the white lie.

Hold the hand of this lie, and take it all the way to the Kingdom of Ends.

My anxiety became as surreptitious as a creepy stalker. Make it to tenure then, go ahead, have that nervous breakdown. You earned it. Finally, rest. Just like in the old days when they'd pack you off to a garden to drink tea with the other patients. Now they call it rehab and you sit in a circle and humiliate each other into degrading confessions.

My focus on this perilous track to tenure gave me no time to fantasize about the reprieve of institutional life.

Other than that one institution: the university.

As an analytic philosopher, I understood relational facts, causal facts, implications of these facts, facts about nature, and mechanisms of the brain.

We have to discipline colleagues who step over the line. Although ambition can also breed high achievement, as attested by our university's own triple-a mission statement: Aspire. Aim. Achieve.

We coddled the pathetic adjunct. A malingerer. Not ready for a full faculty slot.

Then further undermining LeBec's credibility, Tanis told me that she had pasted full body shots onto websites linked to our department, along with lists of praise that her work had evoked from eminent scholars.

"Check it out," Tanis told me. "It's like academic porn."

"If I'm going to watch porn, I don't want the word academic in there."

At the end of our hall, students and colleagues whirled. A vortex: tiny, tight, and alert.

I pushed through. In the eye of this tornado sat LeBec.

Her skirt hiked up along the muscles of her thighs.

Her body parts cantilevered in ways that required a tulip's focus.

She sucked pensively on her tongue ring.

Whereas I wore the same three suits in rotation from Forever 55.

To the students she said, "Call me Helene."

Whereas they called me Professor, respecting our professional disparity.

Any moron could understand LeBec's draw for faculty and students. Procreation and recreation equal the cycle of life.

LeBec had no bones under her pedagogy or research. One day they will sheer it away and leave her skinny, naked, and trembling by the side of the road.

Even though you are not the popular choice for marketing researchers, your time will come—the outsized, the mentally ill, the personally degraded, and the old, whose skin tears like tissue paper more delicate than a perfectly intact hymen. Mine, an heirloom to be cherished and folded into its original box.

And then weighing on the delicate fabric of my situation, I had the additional pressure of LeBec—that adjunct of the seven languages and the twenty territories—perched at the end of the hall, watching for my spot to open—my F-slot.

Then during one of his check-ins, Denke paused at my door.

"What do you think of LeBec?"

I didn't want to feed his obsession. But he was staring and expecting something from me. Reaching within to find some tiny cogent gift, I pulled out only what I'd heard attributed to LeBec in the hall with a single word: "Stellar." Denke smiled as if I'd just confirmed his opinion, then trudged beyond me up the hall.

THE AUTUMN RAINS came. The students scurried along in their slickers and boots as LeBec eyed me more closely. No one to tell about the stairwell person. Not even Tanis, now unrecognizable from the person who'd pulled her plastic tray up to mine in The Perk.

I'd always sat alone. My colleagues paired off or clustered

in groups. Tanis was single, childless. We had that commonal-
ity. Beware of your brand! It could become blighted, lackluster.
Optics is everything. Remember the one scoop rule. One is
good. But two is one too many. Diversify. Have some fruit on
the side. Or chocolate.

Tanis and I were the same size and exchanged opinions
with a flat, bitter disdain. People sometimes confused us, calling me Tanis, or, Tanis, Del, or sometimes even Deltan, the
opposite of the beautiful Hollywood naming couplets adored
by the media, or even worse, as if we'd fused into some blob
thing, a kind of radioactive Fukushima horror creation. There
our similarities ended. Tanis was as plain as a barn. A political
philosopher. Wore clothes patterned with cartoon animals.
Overcompensated, dredging up a chipper proficiency, a highly
valued commodity in our department of the dour and con-
templative. She once confessed that she used sentimentality as
both salve and sedative. We didn't call attention to each other's
failings.

As the esteemed John McGilvery would have exhorted,
"Do not reveal others to themselves. Most can't tolerate the
truth and will soon grow to hate you."

McGilvery had no friends. One academic had stated that
when he'd told McGilvery about the death of a mutual colleague, McGilvery responded with a criticism about an article
in the most recent issue of the *Journal of Morality*.

He probably said it with the exact same flat demeanor he
used years earlier when he said, "Christ, Del, nobody died."

The day Tanis first approached me in The Perk I'd pinched
my mouth to deflect my inevitable disappointment and rejection. But with the fluorescent lights pinging off her broad,
doughy face, I sensed something genuine from Tanis.

It was our first of five lunches and we even hung out once at night. I considered Tanis my only real friend in the department.

Tanis fingered her tuna fish sandwiches and those slim chocolate Rob Boys as we discussed faculty in small derisive ways. We bonded by the razor-sharp garrote, the piano wire of our animosity and insecurity. Our reflections changed in the cellophane wrappers. Once again, I was reduced to the table of misfits, outcasts, and losers.

But at least now that loser was another academic.

Progress!

We teetered on the verge of Halloween madness. The masks, firecrackers, pumpkins with jagged smiling faces. Kalli pinned a fascinator to her hair in the shape of a witch hat and handed out tiny twists of candy. Some idiot stuck gum to my lectern, so I had to spend the night icing the pages and picking it off my notes with my fingernail. Meanwhile, I had my own monster to contend with. He coiled tight. While I stood in the hall, I angled my eyes just enough to know he was there. Alert to my presence, he acknowledged me, tilting his head in my direction. Danger! He'd provoked me, but I wouldn't let on. As far as he knew, I still hadn't seen him. Don't think about it until after tenure. They were meeting. Although, nobody had told me when.

I will defer to the wisdom of the LEAP Seminars, typically recommended for the challenged faculty:

Learning Education Aptitude Programs.

Learning Education for Academic Progress.

Limping Entertainment for Asshole Professors.

Lamb burgers Edible by Alabama Porkers.

Those seminars they required me to attend. Me, but not LeBec.

In September, Denke had signed me up against my will.

"Humiliating," I grumbled to Tanis, "Like the Special Olympics for academics."

"Except you might want to take out the word like," said Tanis. "And FYI, nobody will be leaping in those seminars."

"That's good. I hate exercise. Legs are wasted on me. Give me WiFi and let me bob around in a vat of Old Milwaukee."

"I heard they give you candy."

"FYI, I can buy my own candy."

They did give us candy. A dish of jelly beans glittered at every table.

An eager pair of blond twins (not real twins) with glossy pony tails, peppy voices, and dewy resilient skin held us hostage with a laser pointer and slide show.

Must be what it feels like in prison, earning points for good behaviour.

I ate their candy. Completed the training, faking a pleasant attitude.

"Wow, Del, you're like our poster child for LEAP," one of the twins said, handing me a certificate of completion.

According to LEAP, one must expect to deal with the difficult faculty or student. Do not give false hope. Navigate passion. Maintain a rictus of grim equanimity, so they will accuse you neither of disrespect nor disobedience. Abide by a statement of principle: A respectful, safe environment, both the mantle and pivot of our institution.

I had too much to lose. My apartment, my queen-size mattress, my new twelve-hundred-dollar couch from Planet, my library. I arranged my books by height. Colour. The philosophy books. And the other category, which included everything else.

Do not use a rational being as a mere means, or you won't enter the Kingdom of Ends. It sounded like something Pastor Kevin would've said, *Let's all join hands and enter the Kingdom of Ends.* Is there really such a distinction between philosophy and religion? I often wonder whether they are an outgrowth of the same human need for some kind of external moral structure, so that those who once needed it always need it no matter what the *it* is. Sometimes I wonder if the inner need for an ideological structure explains why some very religious people slide over into conversion or cults whereas others don't. Maybe the more rigourous and demanding the ideas, the more analytic the mind, e.g., moral philosophy may require a more analytic mind than, say, some UFO cult. However, I haven't read the latters' thesis. Unlike Tanis I saw such needs and their corollary of sentimentality as a scourge, not a sedative. What was meant by a "mere means" anyway? Something I would use only for my own ends? Was I supposed to apologize every time I used anything as a mere means? Was I supposed to apologize to every fucking asshole I offended? Tonight, I will make my apologies to my carrots and toilet paper. As well as to that empty bottle of Black Label.

More than once the stairwell person tried to initiate eye contact. I became aware of his obsession with me. Still, I would not acknowledge it. Nor turn my head.

I studied him with a glance perfected with my esteemed mentor who hadn't liked me looking directly at him while he sat at his desk, contemplating universal morality. Just as I didn't like the stairwell person to look at me. Although, I now theorized that he may have been a dark distraction rather than a danger. Neither criminal nor malevolent be. My professional assessment: disadvantaged. Emotionally compromised. A psychiatric patient who found refuge as he stared at me between the fronds of his hair.

The building had been abandoned. He thought he'd found a spot, and as with any biological organism, wasn't quick to give it up. Seemed to understand the rules of engagement. If I turned my head, he moved back inside a shadow. Fungus responding to light. I held the power to report him. Two opposing forces co-existing in nature.

I LECTURED ON Mondays, Wednesdays, and Fridays. But two months after I first saw him, the stairwell person was still always there. The corridor to the basement of John Kenneth Hall was black and shiny with a floor of tiny specks of colour that looked as if it were trying to imitate an expensive exotic stone, but was really meant to distract the eye from the scratches and scuff marks. It was spotless because it was abandoned and hollowed out like an old war bunker. If I got trapped during an earthquake or some other disaster nobody would come looking for me.

Then I began to notice the appearance of wax cups and plates, pleated as if someone had made thumbprints along the edges, and Styrofoam containers literally melting away from a red sauce. He waited for me, groping me with his eyes.

John McGilvery's eyes had scanned those other girls from my residence at Mary Seaman Hall, skin tight and shining with hope. They always sat together as if to draw attention to their genetic superiority—like they needed to oversell it!

John McGilvery, my esteemed professor, narrowed his eyes, calculated. Paced territorially up and down the aisles of the massive theatre. Taught History of Philosophy. Beyond the blue blossoms of cigarette smoke, the windows clenched against the frost outside. His eyes slowed to take in those more pretty and precocious girls.

Annie Money and I shared a room on campus about ten miles away from Slaughter at Mary Seaman Hall. McGilvery eyed her and her friends one by one as they stared at him, trying to memorize every word that he spoke.

Then night after night at Mary Seaman Hall, they crowded in on me.

"Have you ever had sex, Del?"

The girls glinted, straining not to meet each other's eyes, so as not to laugh.

"So, have you ever been with a man, Del?"

They squinched, almost convulsed behind their hair and hands.

"Men don't like to use condoms, Del."

It didn't matter. Unlikely that anyone would ask me to have intercourse.

I followed rules. Discipline. Inordinate discipline. Me, the scholarship student from Wilbur Smith. Always called the faculty Professor. Unlike Annie Money and those others. They called them John or Bob as if they were talking to boys their own age. They would laugh and hush in tiny, shining clusters. Their glances slid past me in Mary Seaman Hall. Annie Money was tiny, fine featured, a blonde pretty girl with freckles and bright green eyes who wore her hair messy and her jeans slung low on her hips, and strode around campus extruding a hot, predatorial sexuality—the one who said of her professors, "There are ones who will, and ones who won't"—glimpsing over at the other girls, then flashing away.

"And those professors aren't even listed in the undergrad

manual," I called out from behind my book. Silence followed, then the girls erupted into shrieks.

"Del!" Annie Money said as if she was embarrassed, almost angry.

After the others left, Annie Money wouldn't talk to me. Wouldn't even acknowledge me. She sat around with her legs spread, smoking cigarettes, picking bits of tobacco off her lower lip. She didn't wear underwear. Her tight jeans clung to her tiny hips by a thick leather strap. They balled up on the floor of our dorm where she dropped them like a pretentious and antagonistic art installation. Crotch seams caked with degrees of paste. It was gross. I didn't have to answer to someone like that.

Then McGilvery hovered above me as I sat in The Nook, drinking coffee.

"What you said in that paper was somewhat interesting, almost good."

"Really?"

"Really," he said. He imitated me. Smiled. Teased. Almost charmed. Mischievous. "Yes. What was it?" He tilted his head, "'Analysis is the sorrow of the mind.'" He steadied his eyes on me. "I'm impressed."

Then later he slid in the chair across from me.

"Who are you, Del Hanks?" He examined me with a sideways smile. "Your last paper dealing with my idea of the five pointed star is rather good. But what do you believe in?"

"I don't know," I said.

He bought me a coffee in a Styrofoam cup. Slid it toward me as if I'd said yes. I nervously bit little horseshoes into the rim.

"It's great to have someone to finally talk to, Del Hanks. You know."

"I know."

He asked if I would like to be his assistant.

Then he left me there, twisting in that tarnished metal spoon. The next day he found me at his office door. I stood, waited.

"What are you doing here?"

"You said I'm your assistant."

He steered me inside to an old, smudged typewriter. Began to dictate. I found myself typing up notes for his new book, *The Five Pointed Star*, on the IBM Selectric. The tiny ball whirred and spun as I typed, hashing and rehashing variations of the same thought experiments with subtle differences that didn't make sense to me no matter how much I turned them around in my head.

"Let's turn to Kant's discussion of the murderer at the door. Why does Kant tell us not to lie if the murderer comes to our house asking about the whereabouts of his potential victim? What if there are other people in the house that could be harmed by letting the murderer in? What person would allow the murderer in the house? Most rational people would not allow the murderer in the house. Do we lie to the murderer? Do we let the murderer into the house?"

He updated his lists of moral situations and questions, changing one word then changing it back again and again.

I made copies on a mimeograph. He kept two in his office, one locked in the filing cabinet, one in his desk drawer.

It was Friday night. We'd completed a fifty-hour run—a load that had far exceeded the limit for teaching assistants. He contemplated a list of questions, taking them out, making notes, then handing back a stack of handwritten papers for me to type. After I completed the work, I stood at the edge of my little typing table.

"I'll be back tomorrow," I told him.

He didn't say anything. I didn't say anything after that.

I knew about the children, the wives. His second wife Susan had left him. Why would she leave him? What was wrong with her?

The faster I typed, the closer the words made us until they became wet and blurred on the page in front of me.

I could hear his breathing, and the heat of his body and his mouth.

He was skinny. A face as pointed as a rodent's, but brilliant. A young family, but they were gone, dissolved somewhere in the ether. And adult children from another, an older family from a previous marriage.

Leaning back in his seat, he put both feet up on the desk, posing questions to me, correcting my answers quickly, flatly, without a single blue vein of emotion.

It's true I'd worked alongside him in his office, the quiet research assistant. Most of the other professors laughed at him behind his back as he kicked the door closed behind me, me the fat anxious girl with the strange aureole of white-blond hair. In what was to become his masterpiece, *The Five Pointed Star*, I compiled his arguments, defending and then destroying the idea of a universal moral philosophy.

McGilvery distilled the norms of action of all schools of moral philosophy—virtue ethics, consequentialism, deontology, egoism, even nihilism—into one, and in so doing, discarded the need for any of them.

His colleagues argued and debated over whether such a feat was possible. I thought of this even while the word fucker popped and burst in my head.

I spent hours a day in McGilvery's office at the end of the

corridor in Berger Hall, our university's oldest building. He wouldn't discuss research matters. Would rarely talk, preferring to sit and stare out the window.

"Let's return to Kant's discussion of the murderer at the door. What if the murderer was a Nazi and you were hiding Jews? What person would rationally allow the murderer in the house or tell the whereabouts of the Jews? What if we did as Kant suggests and didn't lie to the murderer, but simply pushed a piano onto the murderer and killed him? Would that be a better moral solution? Another option would be to let the murderer enter the house, but then to watch as the murderer and the Jews fought it out. Or would it be preferable to have a tiger waiting by the door, and to wait see who would win: murderer or tiger?"

Whenever I questioned his moral examples, he would become agitated. "The answers come through these thought experiments, but these aren't the true answers. Do you understand? It's a paradox. Nobody can think critically anymore. Your generation is hopeless. I pity all of you. You're all going to die."

"Okay," he'd said a few minutes later. "I will try to explain this to you, but it's futile. Don't interrupt me. Only through tragedy can we understand a world that cannot be understood. A world where no amount of analysis and calculation can provide the answers."

"But isn't that what we're doing?"

He stared at me incredulously. "I can't engage on these terms."

Eventually I stopped asking him. We sat together in silence against the clacking and whirring of the IBM Selectric or the muffles of people outside.

Each day this went on as I kept typing for him until one day he rose from his chair. I typed faster, scared he was going to yell at me, or worse, tell me to go.

THERE WAS NO other route to my remote lecture theatre. The dark hole. The stairwell man clouded at the edges of my eyes. Moving, shifting under his hideaway, the points of his limbs flashing. The dust particles circling him as his shining black points sucked me in. I pretended not to see him, as his eyes still trained on me.

Where was security? Did they not do rounds anymore?

Welcome terrorists!

I would not encourage. Would not turn my head.

But that didn't stop him from trying to catch my attention from under that stairwell between the shards of his hair. It confirmed evidence of a primitive brain. He conveyed his message to me through the eyes. Prisoner. Dolphin. Coma patient. Eyes open. Instruments of examination. Pad of paper. Pencil. Questions. Decipher. This and that.

Two blinks.

Yes, I am here.

One blink.

I understand you.

Three blinks.

Get me out of here. Please, take me back to the real world.

Careful!

He was probably dangerous.

Keep your distance. He'll lash out.

The Committee for Tenure.

Nobody knew I saw him. What you don't acknowledge, doesn't exist. At least, it may not exist. So I never saw him, I would tell them should they ever ask.

I've always believed in reason.

Not like the students who dawdled after class, watching me anticipatorily while pretending to check their phones. I gave them the terse smile that made them slouch out. Nothing made the stairwell person go away.

I am not Freud, but neither am I completely out to lunch. I did have some understanding of the scope and the machinations of youth in crisis.

I wasn't dying to meet with the students, to listen to their mundane narratives. Often relieved to find no signature on the sign-up sheet tacked to my office door. They came. With their cups of coffees and their tears. How could I tell them it would be all right when I myself didn't have the answers? None of us understand the pressure required for the metamorphosis. Nature is violent. The system devours some, inalterably changes others.

He'd have that sour smell. I couldn't help looking back at the black hole under the stairwell. Slouched against the outside wall of the stairwell, eyes shut as if he was asleep. He didn't move. Nobody could sleep standing like that. I stopped. Was he dead?

In a moment of weakness, I shifted my gaze.

He flashed open his eyes. Stared right at me and grinned as if he had something on me. His eyes locked onto mine as a blade of fear cut through me. He raised his fingers, crossed them together. A paraphilic rubbing up against me on a crowded bus. He'd broken our unspoken agreement. I angled a hard look. He squeezed back inside the shadow.

The thought of reporting him slipped between my fingers.

The next morning, I considered my options.

Not easy for the academic to make friends. Shaped by interiority, eccentricity, and awkwardness. Paradoxically, even while drowning in a sea of bodies, every body off limits.

At my welcome-to-the-faculty cocktail party, Blegg had sidled up beside me conspiratorially. "Faculty here don't hang out. What you don't know, you won't hate."

I'd learned I had nothing in common with my colleagues, who seemed gross to me. Might as well have been working as a secretary at an insurance firm. I parsed their comments after every engagement while staring at the walls of my apartment.

I had no real business there. Aside from my job, didn't know anyone: The barista at Grounds for Divorce, ski hat pushed to the back of his head, looked at me blankly without recognition when I asked for the same bag of Irreconcilable Differences every week, ground for espresso. The girl behind the reception desk at the doctor's office who after six years still said, "Are you a new patient?" The parking attendant at the university who never acknowledged me with his eyes as I passed through his gate. The night manager, Neil, who was always talking into a walkie-talkie and had the glazed eyes of the chronically high. My students. My colleagues.

People go to Twelve Step meetings. Meet other people, make friends, fall in love. I wanted to tell a group of strangers the lurid details of my life, but became afraid one of my students would show up and report it to faculty.

We'd acknowledged each other. The damage was done. No going back now.

I had done everything I could to turn my life around from that dank hole in that neighbourhood that had housed our greasy little store and the apartment above.

IN THOSE DAYS in the suffocating swell of Slaughter, I watched my future walk in and out in the form of dead-eyed workers, coming in for beer, cigarettes, jars of instant coffee, or kids buying candy with sticky-fingered money, all the necessities for the apocalypse.

The change blackened my fingers. The tobacco and the dust rose to our apartment above the dirty, grey rectangle, the windows grated by wire. And then even after I'd received my scholarship, she'd eye me from across the store.

"Look at you. You'll come back. They always come back."

"That's never going to happen," I told her.

"It's a man's world. You'll get pregnant," she said in a hard, shrill way I despised, but with a tiny clutch at the end on the word pregnant.

She always acted as if she knew more about me than I knew about myself. Trundled through life, striking at everything with a gaze as aggressive, blunt, and absolute as a hammer, lacking insight into the limitations of her mind.

"It's a tragedy," she'd say. "Mr. Jones died, you know."

"He was old and he died. That's not the definition of tragedy."

"Tell him that," she'd say.

Years later I was able to process that clutch in her voice. It was the fear that accompanies a wish she had for me, and she worried it would never be fulfilled. But back then I, with my own shortsightedness, had interpreted what she'd said as nastiness, and for years I hated her for it and punished her at every turn.

The girls at my high school, Wilbur Smith, were no different from my mother, few aspirations or distinguishing characteristics. Mary got more formal training and became a nurse. Lana Slutsky (aka Lana Slut) smoked lipstick stained Virginia Slims, back teased her hair and wore too-bright blue eye shadow. They all vanished with boys in the alley, their sullen eyes sparking with the wet fevered thrill of having been selected for some mysterious and lascivious purpose. Some boy whispered or gestured to make the girl follow behind him and allow everyone to witness his prize, often to the sneers, jabs, or longing of the others. After, the pair would re-emerge, vibrating, dewy, glistening. The girl would sit in one of two ways:

1) darker than before, cradling and almost in shock, arms crossed over her chest, protecting something that had been broken, or

2) shinier and newly molted or hatched into a more advanced being.

Either way, something occurred that could never be fully understood by anyone who wasn't there. If you weren't one of the two, or maybe a friend or several friends who were lucky enough to get parts of the story, you could only piece together the evidence in frustrated configurations of imagining. But no matter how hard you tried, you would never be satisfied even after months or years of shifting or changing the pieces.

Once taking out the garbage on Slaughter, shadows sawed behind the dumpster. A female voice, breathless, unrecognizable called out, "Fuck off, Del!"

Lana. Jane. Rhanda. Jillian. Sharp featured, luminous watchful eyes, slim delicate bodies systematically reduced and destroyed by seventeen. Jane. Serious, forthright. Studied French and Spanish. High buttoned blouses, long skirts, straight home after school, clutching a book in front of her like a crucifix.

Nobody had sex with me behind a dumpster. Girls stuffed themselves into the bathroom, shimmering in front of the mirror, adjusting their tops, applying Lip Smackers, talking, chirping. Then the sharp flash of a laugh.

"No actual kissing."

"Fucking."

"It's what they really want."

"Cock tease!"

Clustered, flicking back their hair, shining under bathroom lights. Wrangler jeans. Tits popping out of leather vests. Plastic combs. Teeth sticking out of tight back pockets. Wavy mirrors. Camel toe. Coiled blue curls of smoke.

The door cracked open.

"No smoking!"

Cigarettes rushed under cold water faucets.

Love's Baby Soft. Charlie. Peppermint breath spray. And back over there, where no one had known and no one suspected, I sat in the far corner of the long row of cubicles wedged behind a door. The girls shimmered out from that narrow slit as a tiny metallic ball of envy and fascination spun inside me.

On Slaughter, no Annie Moneys or Helene LeBecs. Careful hands transplanted them into universities from rarified enclaves. They vibrated with a dark intensity. These girls focused my world as sharp as a blade. If I tried to touch it with my hand, that blade became a 3D projection that left a sick, icy feeling inside me whenever it disappeared.

Now I'd convinced the world I was a member of this group I didn't belong to. Anxiety picked at me until I blistered with sorrow, self-pity, and sheer amazement at the absurdity of my own shortsightedness and misguided choices.

"You should have worked as a legal secretary," my mother said, with a tight dark glee.

I had risen beyond my potential. Would've been happier as a secretary, like my mother had advised. Over the years, since my time at Wilbur Smith, university, and even now, I had pinched down my rage into a tiny point and secreted it deep inside myself with the other tiny points that threatened to kill me if I moved. I didn't know that to be proficient at something small was superior to struggling at something more ambitious.

Too late now!

I've used up more than half my allotment.

My brother Clint managed to earn a living as some kind of teacher for a while, until he went on a medical leave—now he smoked weed and hid in his room, listening to heavy metal.

He moved in with Stacey, ten years older, an ex-stripper who looked like a barbecued snakeskin and still hung out at the Roxy. She paid the bills and let him live in her basement. She treated him like a high-maintenance pet that becomes anxious if you change its routine.

My father was a small man with curved shoulders and fawn-coloured hair. He learned to invaginate himself just to co-exist with my mother. One day she handed him a cup of coffee, and he threw it against the wall.

"It's too hot!" he cried, trudging back up the stairs to his room.

I once believed that work should be the engine of identity. My parents, their hunched little lives wedged between that store and our apartment, and that sordid glistening moat of Slaughter, floated by with bag people, junkies, and prostitutes.

I had turned my life around from the dim lights glinting in

the darkness. Birth, death, nameless, forgotten, irrelevant, except to those generations that had nudged up right before and after mine until LeBec threatened to suck me back into those dark streets.

II

I WOKE UP to bells and whistles, notifying me to a catastrophe. Up for tenure, I wanted to avoid complications. Hoping for a distant war, a meteor striking a faraway continent, instead I discovered congratulations trickling, then pouring in, from our faculty.

LeBec had manoeuvred herself into receiving our university's prestigious Franklin H. Beeby prize, voted by a wide margin of our student population for the brightest new faculty member. Philosophy had never garnered a Beeby. I knew what was coming. A celebration. A party. My colleagues passed LeBec in the halls with congratulations, high fives and fist bumps for bringing the excitement back to philosophy.

"She's making philosophy hot again!" someone said.

The last time that was really true was maybe at some toga party in ancient Greece. I told Tanis that it was only a matter of time before they replaced our department with something more relevant.

"Like vlogging," she said.

"Or flogging," I said.

Since LeBec's arrival, the students throbbed in our halls with an electric joy.

Many might ask why I should be advanced for tenure, I, and not LeBec, who remained adjunct—albeit a stellar adjunct—?

In a few years she would grow distracted, make a mistake, then shrink, shrink fast, only to be replaced by an upgraded version of herself.

No tenure to protect her.

LeBec had become my trigger word. Her popularity had exploded. She grew brighter as I shrunk ever darker in her shadow.

"Rock star!" several students shrieked out as they passed.

I'd allowed both reason and my senses to betray me. Didn't take it upon myself to understand what LeBec was doing. Now it was too late.

"We must not stop predation. Yes, the animals eat each other, as is their nature. But we must not distinguish our beings from their beings. Just as we must not distinguish ourselves from every other. In this process, we need to acknowledge that we see the animals as we see ourselves: loving, compassionate, ruthless, objectified. Yes, even sexualized. The cow's rump, the horse's tail, the chicken's vent, the sensuous and arched back of a cat. The animals are us, and we are the animals. What we view in our animals, we view in ourselves. Our treatment of them, benevolent or malicious, says more about the way we see ourselves than it says about the way we see them. The pity, the helplessness, the rage, and the despair—that conflation of emotions evokes terror in our own hearts, that we split within ourselves and displace onto the other. It is that very split and separation within ourselves in our treatment of the other when we eat, mistreat, or even love an animal as an extension of ourselves that makes us lose our reason and become, for that moment, insane."

LeBec delivered her Beeby lecture to our department, based on her bestselling and critically acclaimed book, *Animal Husbandry: A Marriage of Convenience.*

A vegetarian, LeBec played a leading role in the advocacy for animals when she demanded only free-range fowl at the chain of Karl stores (I referred to as the Karl Marts—a joke that got at least one laugh from Tanis) and the release of the mice from the laboratory at Roberts Pharmaceutical, which then won her the Beeby.

Around the same time, Denke inquired as to the benefits of my LEAP training. Then asked that I complete the addendum to my curriculum vitae, the lists of my committee work, my other contributions to the mundane bureaucratic tasks required by my position.

I had only a few publications, fewer citations. Sitting in his office, Denke swiveled toward me, pressed the tips of his fingers together, his face creased with worry. Apparently, LeBec's curriculum vitae listed hundreds of citations.

"Get Helene's advice. Buy her dinner."

I had no doubt Denke could sense my repulsion. The idea made my stomach rise. My mouth tightened against the sour taste.

"I appreciate your considering the traction of my research." My grim smile conveyed the essence of my sentiment. "Is LeBec taking the LEAP seminars?"

"Helene doesn't need LEAP seminars." Denke's caustic reaction burned inside me.

Then came the LeBec rumours: this deal or that, headhunters, offers, more prestigious universities.

With an excess of time, youth, and ambition, she exploited the desperation of our students who searched for signs of life in the overworked, dull eyes of the faculty.

Her appearance on the morning news show, *What's Up!* Her image on the cover of *Dish Rack*, positioned against a bed of sharp green blades of grass, eyes glazed, crawling with bugs, so that she looked both sexy and dead. She had two books published, many citations, and so she could get away with dressing like a prostitute.

As the rumours of offers from other universities grew, anxieties escalated at the loss of this stellar young genius and her unparalleled allegiance to our institution.

LeBec knew how to smile, frown, look surprised, concerned, or even interested when people talked. Yet her escalation in our department was so fantastical she might as well have been an alien or a cybernetic clone girl. Her tiny smile convinced me that it concealed some hideous detail about my life. Only twenty something—a fact she liked to reinforce with, "By the time I'm your age, Del" or "Is there a reason you've waited so long to apply for tenure, Del, or to publish your second book?"

My senior colleagues, Thorlakson and Bute, had demonstrated the dignity required by our academic position, quietly making contributions to reputable journals.

Instead, LeBec had joined the ranks of departmental quasi-superstars, finding stellar success by embracing the fringe, like our colleague in the Music Department, who released a project with F#$A#@ and had a criminal record, or the one in Sociology who wrote for *The Lower Zone*, an online magazine, which explores recreational uses of end-of-life medications and other alternative lifestyle options.

Now crowned with her Beeby, LeBec waited for us to expedite her to the first available tenure slot. The headhunting rumours intensified.

She advanced herself to chair the prestigious Academics for Social Change. Her hand reached out to me from her perch. I should have yanked mine back from this person who'd positioned herself as our university's humanitarian and moral philosopher.

WHILE THE NOVEMBER trees grew starkly naked behind the silver beaded rain, the stranger's eyes still glowed darkly in the mouth of the stairwell.

Eventually someone did say, "Have you seen that person living in the stairwell?"

"Nope," I said, dismissing them with a clipped voice and hard smile.

The truth was I didn't know how to respond to that question, or most random questions thrown at me. Later I would wish I had said something. But at the time I didn't know how to rectify the situation without looking like a liar. This had obvious moral implications that could damage my credibility. I was not a people person. I had to prepare myself in advance for any kind of normal conversation. And even then I walked away from these interactions feeling like an inadequate, awkward boob. Academia requires rigourous isolation. I spoke with no one except students, colleagues, and others—doctors, accountants, dentists—who fulfilled a purely professional purpose.

"I'm sorry," said the doctor, slipping his hand under my bra to unhook it before expertly placing the stethoscope on my back.

A doctor's examination table, a gynecological speculum run thirty seconds under warm water prior to insertion, the clinking of change from a cashier's hand, the heat rising off the white sheets as a student submits her paper.

I had never intentionally touched another person. It repulsed me. Any form of physical tenderness tasted like metal, threatened to seep inside. I had to clamp it off before it killed me.

I couldn't tell if people touched me out of kindness, or if

it was the unique thrill of being in proximity of such monstrous banality.

My colleagues thought I was difficult. The feeling had become mutual. I had grown a shell of private antagonism toward them to compensate for my natural shyness and fear, exacerbated by the truth of how I'd arrived here.

Several months earlier, Tanis had invited me to dinner at the Garrote. Wine sloshed from chamber pots. Without warning, and like a curious child with a stick, Tanis probed into my personal life. She must have caught my fear and shock, and changed the subject as if she'd inadvertently said something racist. Her quick retreat offended me. I didn't want to be treated like a freak, roped off with a quarantine sign, or like someone who could only love or be loved by animals, or inanimate objects: table, circus ride, or barstool.

While I wasn't prepared for her inventory, it was the first time anyone had taken an interest. Twenty years ago, as an undergraduate, I had traded any prospect of a real life for letters of recommendation, and they reconstituted me. And while I knew I was an okay student, I was not even close to the masterful genius those letters described.

I *was* an imposter. My academic position was based on a fabric of lies and deception, that began to tear with the application of any sort of pressure. The demands of academia whipped and brutalized me. I considered the life I could've had if I'd just accepted the potential of my mediocrity. "*La petite vie.*" I was over my head. The pressure of perpetuating this lie threatened to suck me in with grief, loss, wanting, loneliness, guilt, and desire. I'd never told anyone. Not even Menzer, my former therapist who I thought of as an unused, but expensive, receptacle.

That night at the Garrote, I yearned to tell Tanis how I'd faked my way in. Some part of me hoped she would blanket me with compassion, maybe even commiserate with a "me, too" or a "we're all liars, Del. I thought you knew that," or perhaps I wished she'd convince me that I wasn't a liar, but some kind of awkward, misunderstood genius.

That night at the Garrote on the edge of that precipice, I became starkly aware of my own vulnerability. It wouldn't take much to push me over. Tanis' sudden attention struck me like an arrow. The pain radiated and bleated like a living creature, unfolding with a strange, unreal exhilaration. This is what friends do, how I'd imagined it would be, so I began to hint bit by bit as to what had happened.

"Ha, ha! What progress you've made, Del Hanks!" Menzer would say.

"Ha, ha! I know, right? Only since I fired you, though."

With the wine warming and loosening the joints and bolts of my caution, it had all come burbling up as I slid all the way over into a new and staggering world.

"There was someone," I told her.

She leaned in. The little flames inside her eyes licked at me.

"Del!" she cooed. "What a surprise."

"Well, I'm not dead."

She lowered her voice and spoke collusively. "Who was he?" she asked, then catching herself with an awkward smile. "Or she?"

I rolled my eyes, then answered flatly. "Someone long ago. At college."

As soon as the words came out of my mouth, I wanted to crawl back inside them. Hide. You are being impulsive. Too late. Too late now. I couldn't stop.

"It was twenty years ago."

"Really?" Her mouth twitched, then snatched at me, "Who was it?"

Nothing I'd ever said had provoked such interest from another person. She teased open my cut and my secrets bubbled out, those I'd kept in a vault of shame, despair, and longing, that I'd turned and examined every night with a religious obsession.

Me and my esteemed mentor. As it unraveled, Tanis tilted forward, her tiny eyes betrayed her greedy hunger for my story. She absorbed every word, nodding with pity and understanding as she took in the full depth and texture of my confession.

Afterward, I sat there at the Garrote. Naked. Pink. Quivering. Fully exposed. My sickening confession bending inside me.

Her eyes withdrew deeply as if she couldn't tolerate my shame and regret and was trying to find a way to fix it. Then looking at my desperate eyes, her own softened.

"Look, Del, we all have problems." She fingered the lip of her cup, confessing the seriousness of her diagnosis. "I mean, I'm done. I don't even want to try anymore."

I felt suddenly overwhelmed by both our confessions.

"What about fighting?" It sounded trite. Stupid. I regretted saying it.

"Tried that. Here's a bold move: don't give a shit. Haven't you noticed what's going on? We're in a revolution between the living and the dying. People want to pretend death isn't even a thing anymore. We're here, fuckers. We're not going anywhere. And guess what? We aren't going to pretend we don't exist. We aren't going to make this easy for you." She took a long moment. "It's as if my life is a pilot for a television series that didn't really take off, and I'm sitting in front of a bunch of asshole studio executives. We're not going to renew for another season. We're cancelling.

Nobody is interested, and I want to say to them, Okay, Fuck you! People are interested. They are interested in me. My life counts, motherfuckers. I am ahead of the curve. One day you'll get it. But it will be too late, and you'll be sorry."

Tanis burned with a strange otherworldly intensity, where heated metal changes from red to blue to white. Through the process of dying, Tanis had become magnificent, glorious, beyond anything I'd known, and I couldn't touch her.

Maybe this is what it's all about, I thought. Our goal is to reach this stage of magnificence, the final phase of our metamorphosis, but few could reach it, even through the process of dying. But Tanis had done it. She was an example to us all.

Tanis confessed that she'd tried everything, including a clinical trial that made everything taste sour.

Then she tightened. Her voice picked up an urgency. "I can't lose my job," she said. "It's all I've got left. Please," she clutched at me, "don't tell anyone about this."

The anxious little islands inside me moved apart.

"I understand," I told her.

We made a blood pact, promising not to divulge our confessions to anyone.

Afterward, I had a gross mash-up of feelings. I'd walked away from our meeting feeling somewhat inoculated, but a tiny hammer beat at the heart of my disclosure. Within one week, Tanis told everyone she was ill, then packed and went on medical leave.

MY COLLEAGUES COULDN'T tolerate me without Tanis. Her presence had cushioned the prickle and crackle of my idiosyncratic personality. My voice escalated in volume, tempo, veered sharply along the edges of what is professionally acceptable. I had to control myself not to insult one of my colleagues in some small pointed way.

But sometimes I still slipped up—as with Blegg.

When I asked her how she managed to maintain her publication record through endless pregnancies, she defaulted to that other productivity: reproduction. She told me she only had time to recycle the same paper repeatedly since babies two and three. I viewed her self-effacement as a thinly disguised superiority. Academia steals our lives, our young gleaming lives, so many of us never marry, never bear children.

Yet some still slipped through the cracks—like Blegg, eyes drained of insight and cognitive function, or Krissy in Linguistics, pregnant, glugging from a water bottle.

Tenure. A new marriage. A baby. Leaves of absence: Maternity, immediately after the tenure approved. Thirty-nine. Surprise! A party thrown by the Linguistics secretary. Pink and blue because Krissy had declined to know the gender. "Thank God," some old hag mumbled through a mouthful of cake. "Because it was almost too late."

Now forty, my pressure to procreate has dissipated. Viewed as a lost cause, a poor candidate, genetically inferior, relieving me of the burden of replication.

My stance closer to Epicurus: minimal pleasure means minimal pain.

People meet in bars. Online. They go out, fall in love, get married, and reproduce, only to pop out another variation of their chum DNA.

As with Schopenhauer's human imperative, I cannot help but marvel at our species and its fascination with the banal reproductions of uninspired patterns.

Most don't consider the serious ramifications of realizing their fantasies, believing they can just stick a coin in a slot and see what happens.

Those mothers with glazed, bewildered eyes, dragging themselves down Slaughter, sour milk darkening and encrusting their shirts, faces weighted and hardened with worry and disillusion. I was sorry for the great unwashed, i.e., those in servitude to a more rudimentary organism, unable to maintain their daily hygiene regimen.

Too late for us born in the sixties to those born in the forties, their lack of choices perverted our own maternal instincts via that resentful, tenacious umbilicalis.

I had often thought of ways to torture my mother. I decided that not to reproduce would forge the deepest cut.

Motherhood is a form of biological warfare. It can kill from the inside out.

I was not inured to the maternal drive. No matter what they said about me. The longing for it still cut and turned inside me somewhere. I once had a dream where a strange man would knock at my door and say, I am the father of your child, and then present me with a baby I didn't even know I had. And once while I sat in a doctor's waiting room, a baby clung to its mother, looking at me with its perfect, staring eyes. A tiny French pastry. Ribbons. Bows. Lace. Curls. Rosebud mouth pursed then relaxed. Nudging closer to me, the mother took her opportunity to torture me as I verged over the edge of the glass of my reproductive potential.

"Do you have any?"

She tilted the baby's face toward me like a mirror.

"I wanted to."

Her eyes curved into a question mark of pity, hungry for

my confession, the horrible, jilted love affair that had devoured my fertile years.

"But I was born without a vagina."

Sensing my insanity, she clenched her baby and twisted away.

The perfectly rational mind leaves no room for motherhood.

UNFORTUNATELY, I INTERSECTED the department hallway just as LeBec and Blegg clustered together in that cluckish way. I tried to stride away and avoid, but they sucked me in.

Women can't stop meshing over this one physiological process. It's like we're all supposed to rejoice when we go to the toilet.

Blegg pulled out a snapshot. Her latest tiny monster, dolled up in pink lace and bows. Made me cringe with a pang, strobing back and forth from the past to the future.

"Oh, we're doing that now," I told them. "The next thing you know we'll be pulling out pictures of our dogs and cats."

They waited for further comment, determining my level of pathology in relation to how I negotiated the tragic outcome of my life.

It's important to be polite, to indicate collegiality, even over something as banal as a biological function. I concealed my repulsion.

"Wonderful!" I said as chipper as one offering a blurb for a book jacket cover.

Wonderful! While my own future gummed up in the dirty ball of my past. Nothing could grow there. Nothing ever would now.

DURING OUR MIDTERMS, I could touch the frantic jagged wheels of anxiety even as the students buried their heads in their study carrels. And day after day he still waited for me under the stairwell until finally I could see only the dark velvet of that hole.

He's gone! Gone! I thought.

Well, that's that then. Problem solved.

But as I stood there staring into those dense layers, I bled with an intense sadness. What was wrong with me? Tenure! Move your feet. March! March away to a new future! What future? A different future. One marked by the endless passing of same days, same nights. A wet, dark sorrow weighed me down, and I couldn't move until the little engine of rage picked up again. What had it all been for? Why did I care? Why him? This stranger? What elusive promise could he hold for me? From the distance across the hall, I strained to see inside that lush hole with all its strange potential, willing something to happen almost like a child would will something, until his face rose from that place like a bas-relief. Hoodie, ball cap, the face, noble, as if etched into a coin. The dim yellow light broke. Scattered.

"You aren't good with moral ambiguity. You're in the wrong profession." Or so Menzer had told me. The one with the white beard and Friar Tuck hair I had paid $200 an hour to tell me my problems.

I said a few words that crossed the line of professionalism. Then fired him after he said, "You're crazy! I can't help you." All while he was watering his plants.

IT WAS TOO late to report the stairwell person. If they asked me how long I'd known about him, I'd say, I don't know, a few hours.

My file was still before the Tenure and Promotions Committee. But nobody told me when the committee was to meet. Do not ask. Do not appear desperate. Form a tiny, deferential smile whenever you acknowledge your colleagues. Keep your part of the mechanism alive. Do not allow others to dismantle you, as might well be happening right now.

This sliver of fear embedded itself. It grew inside me. My numb mechanical existence grew the more that LeBec gained departmental prominence.

The moment she twitched into our department, I knew exactly the kind of threat I would be dealing with. Over the years my senses had grown alert.

Each of us has our own unique antagonistic force. In my case, I couldn't escape the menace of the superficial. Children of lawyers, doctors, Republicans who'd gone to school with the Jaggers and watched McEnroe at Wimbledon, supported Reagan, bought the same cashmere sweater from Benetton in every colour.

These blue-tinged anorectics. Tight, tiny chests. Sharp, clicking hips. Hair snapping. Sun incubating within each. Each from one of the ten wealthiest families. Small return on those investments! Boys, hormones raging, oblivious to the value of intellectual gravitas cultivated by the older man after years of wading in the shallow end of the pool. These boys followed those girls with libidinous eyes, turning and smirking lasciviously.

The glorious anorectics secretly appraised one another.

I, conversely, was an outsider. A marginalized loser. Everyone's worst nightmare. I had no money. Did not vote for Reagan. I wasn't even pretty.

Me, the poor scholarship student from Wilbur Smith, raised on an all-American diet of white bread and Cheetos, Chuckanuts and dime-store porn.

One day at Mary Seaman Hall Annie Money appeared, an unusual piece of jewelry inserted into her nose. I'd never seen such a thing and instantly coveted it. A morose, servile woman, a type of servant or nurse, trailed behind her, collecting a few things before they vanished.

Here via Annie Money, I'd witnessed the life cycle. That semester, night after night, perched behind my book, I feigned disinterest, yet was secretly enthralled by the crystalline urgency that played itself out through her perfect body. The tube for the mouth that pumped in lifesaving nutrients. Months later, the same woman took Annie Money away again. Later, she would describe it to her friends with a spring-breaker's brawny exuberance.

"They just sucked it out."

I know they must have inserted her with another lower tube, carrying a little life away into a pail. The tiny prokaryote, its caressing tendrils, flushed down the toilet to transcend our meek world, its strokes more ardent, intentional as it burst into more pixelated waters.

For the sake of accuracy, from behind my book, I added, "With a tube."

"It's not a tube, Del! God!"

A hunger clawed inside me. I yearned for some lurid and voluptuous story of my own. Some dark confession that could

hold the rapt attention of a group of bored, entitled, and precocious little bitches. Gradually, through my isolation and
loneliness, I cultivated the power of envy as an agent of trans-
formation.

Once in Mary Seaman Hall, while Annie Money slept in her
little bed next to mine, the light filtering through the blinds
made her skin so white it was almost cyanotic. Through a re-
fraction of light, she turned into a bird. It spoke to me and said,
"If you recognize beauty here, you can recognize it in yourself."

That day I convinced myself that I too was an entitled little
bitch. A dog barked. A group of big, ungainly frat boys in
striped Lacrosse shirts with long hanging arms kept barking and
laughing until the white spark brightened, then fizzled, leaving
nothing inside me but a hollow ash.

Annie Money and those other girls laughed and flashed,
competing for McGilvery's attention as he scanned the lecture
hall. But in our residence, their eyes darkened, grew private,
troubled, mysterious while they whispered and worked out
complicated problems, usually involving sex and boys.

"You're his assistant, Del. What's he like?"

"Nothing you'd understand."

"Don't even ask her. She's, you know," widening their eyes
like code because they couldn't come up with a word for anything that didn't involve sex. Limited to what they learned in
private schools, country clubs, and trips where they fucked
their way across Europe.

They'd hang around smoking cigarettes, brushing each
other's hair, glancing over at me, lips pressed together, so they
didn't laugh. You could have turned them upside down and
watched their brains jangle out. Tangled, coiled together on
Annie Money's bed, whispering, grooming each other like cats.

I stared hard into the pages of my book, dreaming that one day a stranger would tell me that I couldn't accurately assess my potential and that I was beautiful and special. The black letters would blotch together, forming strange shapes that I couldn't identify on the page.

"Del, could you not, you know, listen?!"

"Don't stare, Del! God!"

"She's so gross!"

I kept my face stuck in my book. Had nowhere to go. Didn't feel safe, wandering around outside in the dark with the rapists. I wondered if Annie Money and those other girls really wanted me to leave or if they just enjoyed torturing me.

McGilvery had once deftly scrutinized those girls. After The Nook, his eyes landed on me. Stayed fixed on me. Spoke to me, directly, through the entire class—me, the scholarship student from Wilbur Smith, the gold medal winner. You intrigue me. You are the only one intelligent enough to get me. He seized me with his eyes as he delivered his lecture, as though I were the only other person in the room.

WEEKS BEFORE THE end of our Fall term, the students and faculty surrendered to the final throes of exams and term papers. I trudged on with my classes. Watched my Introduction to Philosophy students take their seats along the graduated floor at John Kenneth Hall. My tenure application, Helene LeBec, and the stairwell person swirled viciously. I held each thought straight. My hands clenched the lectern. My students happy. Nothing lodged against me. Not a single complaint.

Be careful.

I needed one more year. To proliferate, to advance, to get a publication deal. Citations. I worried that my file might not really be ready. Maybe the reference letters weren't strong enough. Those references letters. The black hole around which all my hopes and dreams swirled. Swirl now. Down this dark drain.

I began to suspect for real that Denke had asked me to go up early, so LeBec could take my F-Slot. I had no hard evidence—other than his moist salivary gaze like someone staring through glass at a cake shop or peepshow.

Even still, Denke checked in with me once a day, as steady as a pulse.

The adjunct picked me out from the herd. Zeroed in on me for some yet undetermined purpose. The skilled sociopath befriends her target.

Over the weeks since the announcement of the Beeby, LeBec's footing had become more confident. Her recent focus on me, her hard, blue doll eyes, her tiny smile, complicated my thoughts. A metallic fear the consistency of tin foil formed in my mouth and lined my skin. She no longer vied for my approval. Her eyes widened enough just to betray her delight and contempt when I did anything to reveal my vulnerability—what she perceived as my professional incompetence.

LeBec's scrutiny and contempt made me wonder if *The Catastrophic Decision* was actually good or actually really, really bad. But as John McGilvery, my esteemed mentor himself had said repeatedly, it's the work itself that does the work. In other words, one must not focus on self-aggrandizement and politics. It's the work. And I returned to that work again and again. Don't be so self-deprecating, I told myself. Believe in yourself, I told myself. But from the Beeby onward, LeBec had turned into a celebrity.

My cells attenuated to their task, every organ galvanized for danger. I managed my anxiety by applying myself fully to the manuscript. I had fantasies that my colleagues would rush up to me and tell me how great the book was, blinking with sincerity and maybe even surprise and glistening admiration. But at some point in the process of working on the manuscript, I had to reconcile myself to the fact that it didn't matter what others thought. I had to get it done, and not look like an inept goofball.

The Catastrophic Decision
Cont'd

> How can we best improve the quality of our involvement with other rational beings and maximize the calculation of interests for all rational beings concerned?
> 8. This is the major conflict between two major positions of moral philosophy: Deontology and Utilitarianism.
> These are two distinctly different and often opposed positions to the same moral questions. Time constraints prevent me from delving into the differences between both.
> 9A. Deontologists dream of entering with other rational beings into the Kingdom of Ends where morality is a system that places all rational beings under moral obligation with each other. Not to be confused with God's Kingdom or Jehovah's Witness' Kingdom Halls. Note: more lamb pictures in reading materials of the latter.

9B. To whom do we owe our obligation?

Typically we owe it to another rational being.

Note: What is a rational being?

Subset 1: Who determines rationality, e.g., a cat?

Subset 2: Can a cat determine rationality for itself? E.g., Hair ball. Making bread. Meow. Is the cat aware of its meow, its hair? Is a cat, therefore, discouraged when it cannot hear its meow?

10A. How should we treat another, irrational being, so we can enter the Kingdom of Ends?

10B. Let's look at other irrational creatures, e.g., Dog. Cat. Horse. Tiger. Mayfly. Mayflies live for 24 hours.

How can we calculate that the death of the other is worse than our own death?

Is the Mayfly's life as valuable as my life?

What is the relevant question when dealing with the others?

Can they, these irrational others, be a means to my end?

10C. Let's turn this around: Can I be the means to my own end?

Note: Quick! Find a side constraint!

10D. Maximum good includes my own good.

10D(i). So what's the problem?

AS I CONTINUED to read, I could feel LeBec's contempt and scrutiny pressing down on every word, making my confidence peel back and split open. I couldn't help wondering what LeBec would think of this book and my piss-poor attempts to finish it; she would pity me and maybe even take it upon herself to apologize to my peers on my behalf to make herself look benevolent. I was her diving board. Maybe with her tiny wry smile and her contempt for me she saw something I couldn't see. I had once thought maybe there was a chance I could pull the completion of this manuscript off in time for tenure and land the book deal. Now there was a much stronger chance I was living in a dream world. I had to buy myself more time. I didn't know how to approach Denke about postponing my tenure. I did not invest most of my adult life only to have a child prostitute sweep in and take my job.

During my meetings with Denke, these thoughts infected me, a dark sorrow burrowing its way inside me. This pernicious notion turned, cutting me with fear that grew into a numb rage. If I asked anyone about the possibility that LeBec might be working actively to supplant me, I'd appear paranoid and insane.

For weeks, I cultivated a black urgency to tell Denke I had made a mistake. But the process was underway, and I didn't know how he'd respond.

Still, I fantasized that Denke would revert to the old Denke, the one who'd campaigned for my hire. He'd take my hand in a voice gooey with compassion, almost like a twelve-year-old girl. "Seriously. Oh, my God! I can't believe you were afraid to come talk to me. I—anybody—would have felt the same way."

But when I actually thought of taking action, fear and panic paralyzed me.

That week, Denke poked in his head.

"Some good news, Hanks!"

"A slam dunk?" I made the motion with my hands, a humiliating display, borne of my exhaustion and lack of dignity.

"No. Not quite. Tenure file passed the department committee, though."

I had so far to go before the file landed on the President's desk. I'd made it halfway up Everest, but could still get frostbite and die or have to gnaw off my own leg.

My file continued to sit before the Tenure and Promotions Committee. They were meeting. But nobody told me when my application would go to the next level. I didn't want to ask. Didn't want to appear cloying and desperate.

The more my tenure fears grew, so did the steady presence of that stairwell person, that spark in the dark hole of the department.

I vibrated darkly.

With the after buzz of LeBec's offer rumours, my colleagues whispered in the crevices of our hall about a celebration for LeBec's Beeby, a faculty dinner.

Put a gun to my head. I wouldn't attend. Washing my hair that night, I'd tell them. I had zero interest in watching LeBec mewl and keen, or my colleagues' stupid, sad duplicitous faces. LeBec's veneer. A thin, transparent film of dirt scratched off with the nail of a finger. But how callous and cruel! How masochistic to make us attend. Let's all rub our faces on the sandpaper of our own failure! I was sure none of them wanted to go. They were now avoiding me, had maybe sensed something about which side of the LeBec line I stood on. Or maybe, I couldn't tolerate to think, maybe it was something wrong with me that made them keep their distance.

I opened my closet. The contents looked like the Salvation Army thrift shop. I'd worn the same garments for years, forgetting what had inspired me to buy them. I stared at them with a sad repulsion as if I'd neglected a now-dead pet.

That week I passed by Fruman's; a decapitated mannequin modeled a white dress. Gauze embroidery. Tiny glass beads. Train. The little bow at the back. Flounces.

They must have been working on commission. The salesgirl galvanized her resources. Nodded with a fierce and compelling conviction until I forked over my card.

This virginal gown would be some departure. Rile things up at the office.

"No refunds or exchanges," the salesgirl told me bluntly. She ratcheted my card through the machine as efficiently as someone engaging the chamber of a rifle.

The next day, I angled and burned in the mirror. A monster dressed as a Hostess cream cake. Godzilla dragging through the streets in a bridal gown.

You've lost all perspective. Your brand is ardent mediocrity and lack of imagination. If you try this, people will laugh at you.

I wanted to cry. Then hung the dress in the closet.

"Look at you. Just look at you. Letting that dirty, nasty loser get to you," my mother would have said.

"A mistake," McGilvery would have said.

"Pathetic," my mother would have said.

But it was my life.

It wasn't too late.

I was only forty. Still young.

Still had my whole life ahead of me.

There was still time. Anything could happen.

$40 = 50 - 10$.

Don't get involved in anything.

It would be ill-advised, John McGilvery would say. One had to be careful. One didn't want to take risks. Even minor ones.

The stairwell man slivered and twisted, something dark deepened inside me, binding him and me together between repulsion and excitement.

I looked in on him. My apprehension bordered on fear.

Know thy enemy.

You might want to get that checked out, they might say to me.

What? My insanity?

Oh, I will, I would tell them.

It's at the top of the To Do list. After this, this, and that.

Between the beats of my repulsion, a dream scratched up. In a field of white flowers, he walked toward me, with each step the thorns pricked him until he turned red.

I am an analytic philosopher. I have no interest in irrational thinking. The results of an untrained mind. I see only what is real.

The mentally ill gravitate toward the magical. They need the shimmer to soften the harsh light of reality. I like reality. It's invigorating.

But now this stranger intersected my sleep after three months as predictable as the rain in this wet, green place, in that hole under that stairwell at John Kenneth Hall.

DURING OUR SECOND last week before the Christmas break, as I made my way to class, I found myself wading through a dirty plastic garden of take-out containers. A finger pushed down inside me. This was his feeding ground. He had to scrounge for old pizza, French fries and coffee, tightening with white skin. He brought them back here where illness could breed and proliferate. I considered bringing him a small mesh bag containing little wheels of cheese wrapped in foil and wax.

If you feed them, they'll never leave.

After six years, I'd forgotten the dull throb of my life. As if I had woken up from a terrible encephalitic dream or a suffocating death. As I passed the stairwell, I wondered if he could sense in me the loneliness, suffering, isolation, a marginalized outsider with a gross secret. None of this mattered. Nothing more could happen between us. Not even the merest meeting of our eyes.

Tenure! Tenure! Twenty years.

Walk away! Walk away!

Just then a voice graveled out from the hole, "You know what you did."

I froze in the middle of the hall as if he'd stung me. What did that mean? What did he know? What did he think he knew?

I stepped toward the stairwell, but the hall was crowded and my students zagged between us. It was time for my class. Don't linger. I retreated to the classroom. I could hardly focus on my lecture. *You know what you did,* thrummed in the back of my head. As I spoke to my class, possibilities of what I could've done turned inside me. The dessert cart was full. Too many to choose from. After my class, I was obsessed with returning to the stairwell, but the students dawdled, checked their phones then thickened in the hall, forcing me back to the department.

When I passed the photocopy room on the way to my office, I heard Tanis' voice, weak, translucent as skim milk, pleading my case to Leo Mahon, tall, rectangular, a block with the jagged smile of a schoolyard bully. He always wore Ray-Bans and his cell phone continually went off in meetings.

"You have to invite Del. She'll hear about it on Monday."

"Oh, for Christ's sake," Mahon said. Then sharply, "Don't push me."

"It's only one more seat at the table."

The voices dropped.

Then Mahon sighed, "I'll tell you why. Because life's too short."

Within me, a hollow cry flattened every other sensation.

I sat brooding in my office as Tanis popped her head in, shiny and glued with tiny arbitrarily placed cotton balls or dandelion fluff.

"Hello. I was getting a few tests. Thought I'd drop by."

She flashed her blue hospital bracelet. "Isn't it gorgeous. It's not diamonds, but it will do," she said before she vanished.

A few seconds later, Mahon knocked on my door to tell me the dinner was that night. "I'm sorry," he said, skimming my eyes with a faux-shame. "I thought you'd been invited."

I folded with despair. The space too tight, I had nowhere to move. I wanted to tell Mahon to fuck off, but for Tanis, I felt obligated to accept his nasty invitation.

THAT NIGHT AT Mahon's, a tiny smug smile crept on my lips. I noted the details, so acutely similar to what I'd replayed with dread in my own imagination since I'd first heard the dinner rumours. I was like Tolstoy. I should've been a writer. My colleagues complimented the tiny, stellar genius. Denke so effusive and gushing, I was amazed he didn't ejaculate. I kept looking for Tanis. My one and only true comrade. She finally bustled in late with Blegg. Blegg of all people! I became hot with confusion and fear. Tanis had wrapped her shiny near bald head in a cheery scarf printed with a cartoon mouse with big lips and a skirt, posing with a hand on its cocked hip. Tanis nodded at me.

Blegg, her hand resting on her enormous shelf of a stomach, led Tanis to a chair. As they passed me, I said, "I could've brought you."

"I know," Tanis said. Her voice twisted in a vaguely familiar way I couldn't identify, but left me feeling distant, lonely, and saturated with self-loathing.

"I can drive you home."

Her smile was tiny, crooked, and her eyes flitted over at Blegg.

Fine, I thought. Fuck it. "Okay, I'm here if you change your mind," I said—and wanted to add—if you want to go home with a normal person. But Tanis was gone across the room with Blegg.

The world was now officially insane. Tanis and I had mocked Blegg at our five lunches, called her the Town Crier—not only because she couldn't shut her mouth, but because she cried in a meeting once.

"It's just hormones, you guys!"

But the next day at lunch, Tanis and I couldn't leave it alone.

"She's always pregnant."

"How many is it now?"

"Like a million."

"Socially irresponsible."

"Well, at least there are more criers for the town."

"Like every town."

Then I realized there was no way Tanis would have asked Blegg over me. Tanis was my friend. My only real friend. Blegg must have gotten to her first—like weeks earlier when everyone else in the world, but me, had been invited. She couldn't exactly say, thanks for the offer but I'd rather go with Del.

"Can I ask why?"

"Well, multiple reasons—mainly I prefer Del as a person."

At least I'd be alone later when I wanted to cry in my car. Maybe Tanis knew that about me. Sensed my anxiety. Wanted to give me space to deal with it without driving her home and the pressure of acting normal.

Mahon strutted and puffed, grinning proprietarily. Glass stems protruded between his fingers like hypodermics.

His cell phone bleated.

"Hey, Leo! What's going on?"

"Another Friday night emergency?"

"Maybe he moonlights at the ER."

"It's the only way he can afford to live in this city."

Mahon's wife, Janice, tanned, athletic, blonde blow-out, saggy knees, watched Mahon go up the stairs then rolled her eyes. "I should probably be suspicious," she said, pinching her lips into a smile, "but he never leaves his study. I guess there's always online."

LeBec sat on the ledge of Mahon's fireplace (a spot I'd never consider for fear I'd snap it off) with her new fiancé, the Japanese rock star, Kuroi Inu. Tattoos, silver jewelry, a mop of bleached hair, and a wary attitude.

Blegg shoved a cracker in her mouth. It poked out her cheek until she rotated it. "Rock star," she said, mumbling through her cracker. "From Japan. Save the whales."

I hated people who talked with food in their mouths.

"Thank you for solving that mystery."

"I know, right. A rock star. Totally apropos."

"Of nothing," I said.

I boiled darkly with a strange fury. We deserved a head's up. What about the trauma of being the last to know? What

was next? Pregnant with twins? LeBec plus two and growing.
Like sepsis. Prepare for everything! Expect the unexpected. Do
not get caught off guard. Don't you dare cry in front of these
people.

I sat squarely on the kitchen chair with the sturdy chrome
legs Mahon had thrust under me and listened as LeBec regaled
us with stories at Mahon's brushed steel table. Her small hands
moved over her plate of *oreilles de crisse* with aspic duff, a thick
productive occlusion of mucous or phlegm or the whites of
an egg or human ovum. I verged closer to the precipice of my
tolerance, especially watching Denke and Tanis smile and cajole.
Don't look. Don't even look. I stared at my plate and repeatedly
itemized the week's grocery list: one bar of unscented Dove
soap, milk, Right Guard deodorant (absolute protection with
the illusion of male proximity), Chef Boyardee Beef and Ravi-
oli. Do not cry. Don't you dare cry. LeBec was telling jokes
now. People laughed. Inu grinned like someone holding a giant
lottery cheque. I shifted my focus to the facts: relational facts,
causal facts, implications of these facts, facts about nature,
mechanisms of the brain, until the streets of my thoughts became so narrow, winding, and knotted that they intersected
inside me, compelling me to think of the young girls' tweets
I'd read the night before as I tried to sleep. Who were they
tweeting? An old man who degraded them by having them sit
on the worn ridges of his corduroy lap or a younger man with
stiff muscular thighs? Either way I could go for the corduroy
or the thighs. They'd feel good, especially if you were facing
away from the man and you could wear a dress with a bow, but
no panties. Was that your idea or his? Maybe you were the
same age as the old man. No, younger. Twenties, but looking
fifteen. I wanted to get up and go jerk it in the powder room.

The idea struck me as genius, so flagrantly radical, a high-cal-ibre, punk-rock manoeuver of protest, until it occurred to me they might have a camera in there. It would be just like Mahon and his saggy-kneed wife to do something gross like that.

"So this guy was leaking something from every orifice—blood, vomit, shit, piss—you name it, and do you think he even noticed?"

My colleagues' eyes glinted around the table. Hid behind their hands. LeBec was leveraging the very people she was sup-posed to be helping at Academics for Social Change to buy points, cheap laughs at a dinner party.

"And I suppose you accepted money?" I snapped. "Hyp-ocrite!"

A silence fell. Smiles and eyes flashed across the table.

"I would've," LeBec said after a beat, and not even looking at me, "except then it would've been like working with you guys."

Laughter snapped the tension in half as LeBec assessed me from across the table. She hardened with contempt, forming that tiny glinting smile that she now produced whenever she saw me, alert to the true depth of my vulnerability.

"That was supposed to be a joke," I said. "Talk about bad delivery." I crowed, "Awkward!" Then said, "I'm sorry. I've had a rough week."

Nobody acknowledged me. They tilted away. Denke stared at me with embarrassment and disbelief as if I'd betrayed him.

Tanis curved her eyes and her mouth at me with disappoint-ment and pity. The others had shadowed and turned away, too, as if my presence were now obscene.

I DID CRY in the car that night, and the Monday after the Mahon dinner. It was the final week of term, and our halls throbbed with students and faculty. While opening my office door, I witnessed LeBec, her hand hovering above Denke's shoulder. Too close together. Lips pressed up to his ear. I fingered the old, worn pages of my lecture notes as she whispered to him. They hushed and glared up at me with hard, shiny eyes. I retreated into my office. Don't act so naïve and surprised, I castigated myself. You are not a child. It's not like you have never seen this before. *You know what you did.* What did that even mean? What could he know about me? He just wanted my attention. But the thought grew and festered. A perfect file. A slam dunk.

I wanted to find him and ask him what he meant. It could only mean one of two things. And both those things kept me up. The one was the issue of my former mentor. The stairwell person couldn't have known about that. I had stupidly spilled the beans to Tanis. They definitely didn't move in the same circles.

I cried and freaked out privately in my office. I had obsessed about the comment throughout the weekend. The coalescence of everything—my constant mistakes, the stairwell guy, and LeBec—spun its configurations inside me like the drum of a slot machine. Cherry. Star. Watermelon. Lemon. Bowling Ball. Sniper Rifle.

Hours before my class, I walked past the cleaner in his closet, clattering the supplies on his metal cart. A day like any other, yet the halls were empty. I expected, at the very least, to see the stranger flashing under that stairwell.

Light cast across the mouth of the hole. I couldn't penetrate it, crept slowly, carefully down the hall as I quickly passed the stairwell once. Then twice. I expected his face again to rise out from the darkness. No sign of him. A shadow fell over the hole. From that distance, I tried to peer in, angling my eyes. Was that thick lush stripe within the layers him? If he struck out at me, nobody was here to help. I started sweating. I ran away as clumps grew under my arms like hands.

It was too early for my class, so I gathered up my papers, and walked past the stairwell again. I thought about the man, LeBec, my tenure. This sickening fork. I felt strange and abstracted as if the universe was thrown one centimeter off its axis, charging me with a compelling, familiar urgency, one that had historically led me to trouble as I tried to correct that tension. It was there from that place that I passed by Denke's office. He made the mistake of glimpsing up at me from his computer, and I sat down. I told him that I was having some doubts about my push for early tenure.

He had become uncharacteristically irritated. His square face and jaw had slackened, the muscle wasting and hanging like an old plastic bag.

"I am fully aware this is not an appropriate time for this request."

"Appropriate." He shook his head. Then held his gaze on me as if he saw something in me he didn't like, and that may have changed his opinion about me. "You should have thought about this a long time ago."

The branches scratched along the window.

"I think I went up too early. I'd like to push my tenure back one year."

"Well, it's too late now. Didn't anyone advise you?"

"Yes." I gave Denke a bitter look. "You did."

"You have your answer. But you were advised poorly."

Shock seized and dismantled my brain. "Well, this is obviously a mistake." I wanted to cry. "Is there anything you would recommend I do now?"

The thrust of my voice was too loaded for our conversation. He didn't say anything, staring out the window as the silence lengthened between us.

LeBec somehow beat behind this initiative to extract me from the machine. She had planted a seed of doubt in Denke.

"I'm not trying to be obstreperous."

"You should have said something earlier," Denke told me. "Now we're all involved. Good God, why did you think it was such a good idea to do this now?"

The silence stuck inside me. "Will this conversation affect my tenure?"

He inverted, gnawing on a private dark thought. He became rigid, the shadow of frustration and disgust cast over his eyes. His voice formed a sharp point as if he was trying to stab me with it.

"I think at some point you need to stop doubting yourself."

"I made a decision, and you were there." I looked at him carefully, catching his eyes. "But I think it may have been the wrong decision."

"It sounds like it," he said, perfunctorily.

"Why did you recommend I go up early?"

His eyes and mouth tightened. Then smiled as if struck by a childhood memory. "In my experience there is truly nothing as beautiful as a perfect file. The committee just looks at it, and do you know what they say?"

I'd heard it before.

Made the feeble motion with my hands. "A slam dunk."

"You may want to hold off. Go on holiday. Get perspective."

"What do you mean?" I could hear my voice grow as high and thin as a child's. There was no such thing as a "break." Once the clock was up, it was over. "You sound like you're advising me to go on a leave." I hesitated. "Or leave."

His eyes glinted like two dimes. "I wouldn't blame you if you did."

Denke rose from his chair. Something in my face—a look of shock—must have revealed itself. His hand landed on my shoulder the way McGilvery's had so many years ago. Then, as if sensing the true potential of my insanity, he removed it.

I reached for the door, opened it, and stumbled out.

I dragged my own stupidity behind me like a dead body. Turning a corner, LeBec stood there as if she'd been waiting for me, her smile pinched tighter than ever, as if she'd just discovered something grotesque and humiliating about me.

"How's the review going, Del?" Her voice eased back and forth.

"As well as can be expected."

She took a strategic moment to deliberate, consider, weigh, then zeroed in. "I was just talking to a friend of yours."

Friend? I stood there, tempted to paraphrase Aristotle: I have no friends.

"John McGilvery." Her smile tightened. "I know he means a lot to you."

All my sensations compressed, hardened.

"I don't really know him," I answered.

Her eyes glinted with a nasty curiosity as if I owed her a complete disclosure. "I thought he was your mentor."

"Years ago." I couldn't shut my mouth. My voice twisted at

the end in an ugly, childish way that made me hate myself. I turned away down the long, dark hall.

STRIDING PAST MY class to the parkade, I hunched behind the wheel of my Jetta, dissociated, like the person who wakes up only to discover they've committed murder.

I lost all sense of time. Miles upon miles. The college area, the pink and blue buildings, the downtown, the high-glass rectangles, the residential area, the square houses, the dark-green trees, the boulevards, into the dilapidated area I'd only passed through before with a line of crumpling buildings, slanting against each other.

At the lights a woman blazed past me in a shopping cart pushed by her minion, a tiny girl in a pink dress with a bow. I thought it was a girl, but it might have been a small woman. The creature in the cart had broken, folded-up limbs, but her neck was long and she held her head as erect and glorious as a queen's. She didn't care if anyone saw her like this. I wondered if she'd ever been someone like me with a normal job. I decided that was unlikely. People couldn't go from working at a university to being pushed around in a shopping cart in public unless something horrible had happened to them.

The sun sank lower and lower behind the trees and rooftops. Streets flicked by: Jones, James, Williams, Johnson. I wondered if this disturbing place named its streets after those who had committed terrible acts. As I searched for parking, I felt as though my hypnotic repetition of those names became an amulet to ward off the spirits of the criminally insane. I came to Henry where stood Lurch, a tiny bar. I parked and walked inside.

So rarely did I break from my trajectory between apartment

and university to witness this safari: sharp, pointed faces, skin yawning over bone pressed against the darkening windows. Inside Lurch, people ate startling but incongruous food combinations while watching the decrepitude behind the safety of tempered glass. In vacation brochures, our city promoted itself as a spoiled, pretty teenager without substance. Here the teenager had a twin. Broken. Abused. Skin picked, blossoming into red flowers. We moved back and forth between them, exploiting them both.

I hunched over a glass of wine. The high, thin voice of a little girl cooed through speakers mounted in the ceiling above like the spirula of baby ears. Couples sat at square tables as a single waiter circled them with imperious, insulting eyes.

When I was still at Wilbur Smith, a psychic took one look at me and said, "You will have professional success, but not personal success." I stood there with another customer, a gawky girl who had a recessive chin that made her mouth look like it was in her neck. To that girl, she said, "You will have personal success, but not professional success." We were both sixteen, and didn't know what to do with that information. We stag-gered away, trying to come to terms with the limitations of our futures.

I had never missed a class. By now they must have realized I wasn't coming back. Tomorrow I would tell them I'd been struck by a sudden illness or tragedy.

I'd already drunk three glasses of wine when, at the edge of my sight, a bird startled me in the mirror, a rectangle hanging above the bar.

Hunched there the stairwell man peered at me from the mirror, his hoodie, his backward cap. The orange sleeping bag bunched under his arm.

I slit my eyes at him, and stared back down at my glass.

"If I want five bucks to eat, I'm going to have to blow one of these guys."

"That's terrible." I didn't know what he expected me to say.

"Why? How much do you think I should get?"

The bartender watched us carefully.

The stairwell man stared at me through that long dirty curtain of hair. He tapped his foot against the bar, flicking his eyes around the room.

"Why are you still here?" the bartender asked the man.

"I been waiting for someone. It's a f-f-free country."

"That's enough," the bartender said. He crossed his arms. "I don't want you here. We had that discussion."

I looked out the window at the pelting rain then back at the man. He was sucking on a tiny ball of paper.

You know what you did.

I turned on my seat to the bartender. "He's not doing anything."

Unlike that adjunct Helene LeBec who might even now be doing something to me as her words about John McGilvery echoed in my head.

The bartender raised an eyebrow and smirked. "Is he with you?"

The man tapped faster, harder against the foot of his stool.

"Fine, as long as that's understood," the bartender said, walking away.

The stairwell man angled his eyes at me.

"Hold space," says LEAP.

The points of his face glistened under the lights.

He watched me, eyes careful.

Then he said, "I had dreams about you. What you think of that?"

"I don't think anything about it."

I avoided looking at him. I didn't want him to touch me. Brush against me. Shake my hand. Bed bugs. An urban scourge. I could've walked away. I could've just paid my bill and left. *You know what you did*. I wasn't leaving without an answer.

Timing is everything. Never rush or force a solution. Stay flat as a mirror.

"But now you're here. It's a sign."

Even after three drinks, my senses were perfectly intact.

"I don't believe in dreams or signs," I told him.

"See, that's dope, though. You get it." He nodded at the bartender. "They don't get it." His fingers tore pieces from a stack of paper napkins that sat on the counter. From under his sleeves, blue and red tattoos bled out, indiscernible splotches along his wrists and hands like an old piece of paper run through the wash.

What I couldn't understand was how he saw past the hair. The triangles hung right over his eyes. He peered at me from between them. Like that one rock star they all want to look like. The one who'd run away from home because he said something bad on YouTube and it ruined his career. I didn't know what he'd said, but according to my students the rock star's shunning was justified. Things were different now. Something like that wouldn't have even been a blip twenty years ago. But that was because of the internet. Now if you do anything wrong your life is over in thirty seconds. But of course that's a good thing. The creeps need to be kept at bay, and there seems to be more of them than anyone knows. Don't look in the mirror! It was like that red candy in the cellophane packets the dentists used to make us chew that showed up the cavities. The whole world was a mouth of rotting teeth.

"Thanks for the muffins."

"What are you talking about?"

It sounded like code for something dirty.

"The muffins you left for me on the floor."

"I would never leave food on the floor. It isn't sanitary."

His fault. I would tell them. He initiated contact.

I calibrated the possible threat to my tenure.

I could envision only the hole under that black ragged stairwell, that long grim hall, the poorly lit yellow lights dangling over the ugly, scuffed linoleum.

"Well, those days are over. Someone reported me."

"What do you mean? Who would do that?"

He shrugged. "You tell me."

I thought about every single person who walked past that stairwell. My students, and Neil, that hippy security guard. I couldn't imagine anyone calling it in.

"I didn't do it, if that's what you mean."

"I knew that," he said, as if it were obvious.

"Well, that's a little presumptuous," I said. "I could've done it."

"Right, that's why you left me your number."

He was probably used to provoking people, and getting away with it. Most people don't even know what they're doing half the time.

"I think you're confusing me with someone else."

The fact was that he was telling the truth. As his image wavered in the mirror, I knew I'd seen it before months earlier. And as I would explain to them, I did leave him my number on a piece of paper. But it was only to help. It was informational.

He lowered his voice. "You know what you did."

I scanned the room to see if I recognized anyone I knew. None of them were members of faculty or students.

"That's stupid. I'd never do that. But if I did do it, it was probably only to help you."

He laughed, looked at me as though he thought I was funny. Rolled little strips of paper napkin between his fingers. Then he shrank and darkened. "Fuck it! I'm the sign of the fox. I'll live in the snow with the raccoons or in the park."

"What park?"

"You real? The woods. Been hanging there now."

"What, that forest? That's dangerous. You can't go in there."

Then he mentioned the trees. *Anciana Madre*, named by the Spanish who'd conquered this area centuries ago. The trees were an enormous cluster of pines. The largest in the area. The parks board gave tours to little children and visitors, but nobody was allowed in the area without an official guide as several students had taken their lives right near that tree in the campus forest. According to local lore, the baroque overgrowth held in its arms the institutionalized, violent, psychotic, and destitute who had foraged, murdered, and birthed children with slow cautious eyes who inhabited that dense black hole. Over three generations of those people had taken refuge there in the forest, one within the other, just as animals burrow within knots and holes of trees. They reproduced in the leaves, turning their dreams inside out from our own dreams, purportedly living within dreams, not of repressed desire and fantasy, but of civilized ritual and hygiene. He wouldn't survive out there.

"It's not safe. You'd be better off in a shelter," I said.

"I'll become a prostitute." His voice grew tight. "I'll deal drugs. I don't care." His leg shook against the stool's leg. "What sign are you?"

"I told you, I don't believe in signs. Your perceptions are different from my own," I tried to explain to him. "There's no systematic process. Dreams are electrical occurrences in the brain. You've got to be rational."

I turned on my stool. "Look, last time I saw you, you said something. I need to know what it meant. What did you mean by, *You know what you did?*"

The door scraped open and his eyes jumped.

"You ever heard of Poolboy? That's the shit right there. That song from Poolboy. 'Clean That Pool'." His fingers tapped the bar. "I'm cleaning that pool. It's empty. My heart, it's preemptive. Makes it all cemented."

He couldn't see past that hair to register the simplest concept.

"Look," I said. "I need to talk to you about something very important."

He became still.

"I know this may seem insignificant to you, but it means a lot to me. I'm at a phase in my life where even the smallest detail can have an impact. Do you understand?"

My eyes scanned the faces at the tables again. I wondered if they could decipher our conversation via our paralinguistic cues. The tables were full. Nobody seemed to notice us. The clattering. Clinking. The joint between this place and my real life.

The low chatter rose with the expectations of the night. It swirled up from the tables around us. Most of the people were young. They had a need to couple. To form a promise to be part of something that lasts forever.

Why did we measure love in time? Twenty years. Thirty years.

Even just a glance could last forever. Not like a marriage worn away by the attrition of constant fights and the boredom and the disappointment of daily routine.

Mayflies live for a single day. Adult males become quasi-females, haunt the edges of streams. Trapped by polished surfaces. Pursued by predators. Included in amber. Burst with intention as they leap from phase to phase. How do we assess the heartbreaking complexity of that single day?

My mother never thought I'd get married.

"It's imperative to maintain an interior logic," I told him. "Analysis is the sorrow of the mind."

He stared at me, growing alert. His eyes widened, absorbing every word. It was so satisfying when they finally got it. When the concepts clicked into place.

"You must know that what you've been saying doesn't make sense. Perceptual states such as dreams are illusions and deliver only putative information at best. I'd like to think they at least managed to teach you that in school."

I could hear the judgement in my voice, and I hated it.

His eyes shot down.

The tiny balls of paper scattered to the floor.

"I should be there now," he said.

He turned inside himself. Grew silent. Dark.

"Where? School? They offer adult education courses at every high school."

He thought for a second, then said, "I don't think they'd let me in there."

"Why not you? You're no different from anyone else."

"I guess not," he said.

Just leave them with one concrete suggestion, says LEAP. Just as I didn't want to interfere with the students. The school admonished me. Not your job. You're not a therapist. Somehow my intentions always became misunderstood.

"Well, at least that's a start. Although, you aren't being very rational about it."

———

"You're right. Life blew up." He opened his hand fast, like an explosion.

His foot crooked at an angle. Something was wrong with him.

He noticed me looking and tucked it in.

"What happened to your foot?"

"Denny started shooting me on my board. I lost my balance and I fell."

I could feel myself gasp. I hadn't expected anything like that. This was a life I knew nothing about. I became rigid with shock, pity, then sorrow. His mouth twisted. He said something fast I couldn't understand that sounded like, "kick bit backslide burn."

"Did you report him?"

He turned inside himself and darkened.

"You have a responsibility to do that."

"No. It's okay. We're friends."

"What do you mean? That doesn't make sense."

Outside the sun tore a hole through the dark sky.

He had seen things I didn't know anything about. Revealed a part of himself. I had to honour that or I'd hate myself. You're a good person. You're interesting, I tried to convey with my eyes. He smiled with confusion, looking away quickly. Then turned his eyes back to me. He opened himself to me. I contributed to that in a way. If I left abruptly, he could do something destructive. I had an impulse to leave him with something productive. To suggest counseling. A phone number. An equation.

I believe in the purity and truth of mathematics.

How many times did I deliberate Sidney's issues with his father or Janice's boyfriend problems? They needed my support. Simon had a girlfriend. Then Darcy, in love, but never reciprocated. You only dream of what you can't have. When fast snacks are available 24 hours, it's not food they need, but the hunger for love. Emails, Twitter, Snapchat, Tinder. My computer nudges, drones, hums next to me in my sleep.

"I think you like me." He smiled.

I gave him a look. "I don't think that would be an accurate assessment."

"Hey, I was kidding. Chill."

When I stared at him, he laughed again then I laughed, too.

"You worried about me, though," he said.

He was smiling as if he wanted to look away, but he kept his eyes on me.

His pale skin flickered under the lights. A tiny blue vein pulsed against his jaw as if that was his heart, vulnerable, but intensely powerful, and he wanted me to see it.

"I don't usually give advice, but in your case, I will make an exception. Expectations lead to disappointment. Are you familiar with the Homunculus Fallacy?"

He didn't answer. Just stared at me.

"Take a package of Sunny Boy cereal, a picture of a boy within a picture of a boy ad infinitum. We perceive ideas rather than perceiving things directly. This leads to the homunculus view of the mind. The regress comes when you consider who might be aware of the perception of ideas—such as a little man inside us perceiving ideas." He fixed on me with a fierce concentration. "Now tell me what you meant by that comment. What did you mean by saying, *You know what you did*?"

He just looked as if he were thinking, then he said, "What came first, the chicken or the egg?" Then after a long silence, he said, "The rooster." He gave me a look as if he was waiting for my reaction then cracked out a jagged laugh.

F is for fail! He was playing with me. He was wasting my time.

Just get up and leave, I told myself. Just do it.

I stood with my bag and jacket.

"Hey, what's up?" He reached for me.

For reasons I still don't understand, I didn't walk out the door. I went to the bathroom and tried to avoid the mirrors. They inevitably led to disappointment. I checked myself as I vigorously scrubbed my hands with antiseptic soap. The chop of dyed black hair, the weird white glasses, the pores that gaped back with red, angry mouths. The prolapsed neck bunched like a tiny sack.

"Look at you. Just look at you, hunching like an old woman."

"Well, at least I'm still alive, unlike some people around here."

I leaned against the sink. LeBec, Annie Money. The burden of being pretty. Life must be tough! I angled my face in the mirror. So hard to assess one's own aesthetic merit. The glass warped and curved, resisting my gaze. I conducted an inventory: nose, mouth, breasts, vagina. I buckled with sadness. Nobody had called me pretty in my entire life. It didn't matter. Nothing would have convinced me. I deflected compliments. Reconstituted positive reinforcement as sarcasm.

You know what you did.

Maybe just something people say to people nowadays, an expression like, What's up? Maybe it didn't mean anything. Maybe he just wanted attention. Maybe the button of his pleasure was the high contrast between my haughty young self and the more desiccated current self. Many undesirables wait until their physical "types" ripen, so they eventually fall from the vine into their arms.

He would be waiting forever.

He had to be at least half my age.

How long could a middle-aged philosophy professor hold his attention?

He would be gone by the time I got back.

You know what you did.

Now I'll never know what he meant.

I'd had too much to drink. The little tables thrummed. The lights and colours streaked and vibrated. My plan was to walk out the door, to get a cab, to go home, and return the next day for the car. When I passed the bar, he was still there, angling and glinting in the darkening light of the mirror. He seemed changed. More muscular than I'd remembered. Face darkened with stubble. His lashes were rising and lowering slowly behind the sharp triangles of hair. How could he see behind those bangs? I wanted to reach out and move them.

He seemed preoccupied. Serious. Pulsing and alive, as if nerves lined the inside of his skin. He said, "Don't you believe something happened to bring you here?"

"You're talking about cause and effect," I said.

"Maybe that's what you call it."

"No," I said. "That's what it is."

A chair scraped against the floor. His neck went straight as a wire. His eyes shot toward the door. Then he relaxed, balling up more paper.

"What's wrong?"

"Nothing," he said. "I have the same dream about you every night."

"I told you, I don't believe in dreams. Not in that way."

"I knew it was you as soon as I saw you. And now here you are."

"You don't know me."

The mirror shivered at the edges of my eyes just as it did that first time. We were in direct opposition to each other. I was short, squat with a face pinched in perpetual dissatisfaction. An aberration in symmetry, but harbouring a reasonable, functional person. His traumatized personality inhabited a beautiful face. This striking realization sped up a tiny wheel of panic. He had changed in that moment; the angles of his face had shifted and caught the light like diamond facets. The long, black hair contrasted sharply with his skin. The composition even. Proportioned. The Golden or Divine Ratio. As perfect as glass, enhanced by his distressed clothes. He looked old. Young. Shimmering. An unstable image. As an ordinary looking person, I have become alert to the beauty of others. My own wish for it worn away through repeated rejections, the lack of enthusiasm in the gaze of others. Our incongruities were obvious to everyone. Nobody wanted us. We didn't belong anywhere, but in that tiny square.

In the past number of years, I'd rarely seen a live male body except for quick, noxious flings (few enough to count on a hand with three amputated fingers). Nothing to write home about. The episodes were largely humiliating and left me feeling (gnawingly in one case) repulsed and swearing to devote myself even more to my book and a life of pornography—the latter both an undervalued and truly satisfying relationship for the myopically narcissistic—crazy, deviant, quick, and dirty—as long as I really don't think about the other person. How they got there, and how they felt about it, exploited, etc. etc. People say it's degrading and lonely, even for the user, but I don't see it that way. That was a functional relationship that could have gone on for years.

His foot stopped.

He glanced away like he was touching something gross, and held it with a flimsy unstable smile. His eyes squinted up, then intensified into a tight, black star.

"She—she doesn't get me."

A hole tore through me. And a wad of Kleenex occluded the hole. Everyone but me had a second half even if it was out to destroy them. I burned with self-pity. Don't make everything about you. His pain has nothing to do with you. Open yourself up to something bigger than yourself. There is no division between your pain and his.

"How long have you known her?"

He kept his eyes fastened on me. "It feels like forever," he said.

He kept sucking on the tiny balls of paper as the rain pattered against the window glass. "She's nothing like you."

A thrill escalated inside me. I tamped it down.

"Well, I don't know if that's good or bad," I said.

"This bitch is a psycho. She runs a fucking meth lab. I've wasted my life."

He jerks the neck of his T-shirt down. A white patch of raised skin, a positive relief, an intaglio like a cameo.

"See this shit," he said.

He let the shirt go. His eyes crackled with bits of broken glass.

"Fuck all that," he said as if he'd just woken up. "I'm going to live in the park with the raccoons." He stared at his shoe. His sock hung half off his shot foot as he sat on the edge of his stool.

He went on about the dream. Those hot sharp circles turned and spiked with messages he claimed he received about me.

Messages about a black hole. It was going to suck us both inside. He had to warn me, so we could both do something about it. "That's why you came to me," he said. "Tonight."

"You can get help from someone qualified in dreams. I can give you a number to call. You can talk with someone at Covenant House."

His voice became impatient. "I think about you."

"These are neurological manifestations. For the last time, dreams are only electrical occurrences in the brain."

He slanted toward me. His eyes welled and his voice picked up a sudden urgency. "I think about you all the time."

I had to take a different tact. "Thinking and knowing are distinct and separate processes."

"I don't care about that shit," he cried. "You know what I'm on about. I thought you were different. You said you liked me. I thought we were friends."

"I use that word judiciously."

"Promise me," he said.

"I am a philosopher. We are precise about language."

"Promise me," he said again.

"All right," I said. "I'll promise as soon as you tell me what you meant when you said, *You know what you did.*"

"Promise me, and I'll answer it."

He laughed again. A cute game, but it made me mad.

You can't have two weak people in a livable situation, my mother would say. It takes a strong woman to turn a man around or a strong man to turn a woman.

He needed help. I would take him to Covenant House. Teach him to talk, to dress. Didn't the hair bother him? Wouldn't he want to swipe it back? It didn't make sense how he even saw to walk down the street. He eyed me from behind the hair. It had become a kind of taunt or lure, the eyes of a wild cat hypnotizing me between jungle fronds. Cut those bangs. Or maybe just move them to the side of his face. A side part. Encourage him to read, maybe even to finish high school. A community service.

I could still have just walked away. I could still have just paid my bill and left. Walk away! I screamed inside my head. What are you doing here? Walk away!

My students dissolved at the edges of my memory. Who were they? I didn't even know them. I might as well be standing in a box talking to myself.

I sat with my eyes closed, trying to think of what to do. My thoughts smudged like the tattoos on his wrists. It was hot. The music was gone. I had gone in too deep. I felt scared. An urgency escalated.

"You're playing games with me now."

"I'm not playing games."

I could feel my hands pushing up against the table.

"I'm afraid our time is up."

His eyes darker blue than the almost black blue of the dark sky. Glinted and silvered and sharpened from the light. "It's closed now."

"Don't be ridiculous." I broke my gaze. But he was right. The place was empty. The sign was turned on the door glass. The chairs upside down on their tables.

I stood up. The bar tilted.

He jerked his chin to the door. "Let's go someplace."

I paused as if he were a friend saying it. As if this was normal.

"What are you talking about? That's not going to happen."

The hair was intentional. He was trying to provoke. I wanted to swipe at it. To push it back. To pull out a lighter and set his bangs on fire.

"I just want to talk to you. I don't think it's a big deal."

"What is it?"

"I can't do it here. Let's go to your place."

"Are you crazy? You're not coming there."

His eyes became sad and scared and trembled.

Despite my excellent credentials, the room continued to spin. Coffee. A taxi. I couldn't drive like this. "I need to call a cab," I said.

"There's no cabs around here."

"That's idiotic. There are cabs everywhere."

I wobbled. I almost slipped, but caught myself up against the bar.

"I'll help you get home," he said.

"I have to pay this bill. The bartender was just here a minute ago."

"He leaves me to close up. He trusts me."

"He didn't trust you before when he was trying to kick you out."

He laughed. "That's just Bobby. He was just playing around."

The bartender must be in the back, having a cigarette. A red brick wedged in a crack between the bar and the alley.

I looked to the door. To the kitchen.

"I have to pay the bill," I said again. My voice sounded fake, as if I were trying to convince myself of something that wasn't real.

"They aren't about that. They're cool."

"Nobody would forget about the bill. It doesn't make sense. The economy!" I said. "This isn't the eighties. Interest rates aren't eighteen percent."

Would they really leave us here? Would they forget we were here? I'd fallen asleep on a bus once. When I woke up, it was dark, and I didn't know where I was. I led myself out of the bus by pushing on the door, trying the door when the sign said *Push* not *Pull*. Why did I keep pulling the door? I was always doing this. Why did I walk against lights into traffic? One day I would be run over, and I'd have nobody but myself to blame. Eventually, the bus door sighed open, giving way as they do in case of fire or accident. And now here I was, and it didn't matter if I'd ever got off that bus. It didn't matter if I'd burned on that bus or if I contracted a disease through my blood intersecting with another person's blood in an accident in the future that would now never happen. I had an ordered, responsible existence. The drive home. Dinner and coffee while I attended to my work. A postdoc. One of the top students at Wilbur Smith, a Fulbright, a PhD, a Folding Chair. I subscribe to sleep hygiene. I read instruction manuals as if not to do so would result in a tragedy that could be avoided through more prudent action.

That dark edge inside me crumbled faster now. What would the faculty say? I had gained a respectable job. A position. Accomplishments. Martin Baumgartel, in his review of *The Real and the Unreal*, had referred to my will, my determination, my strength of character in creating this book, "A work unparalleled and boundlessly syllogistic and peripatetic." Now I wondered if Baumgartel meant my work was too confusing, but had found a more intelligent way to insult me.

As I sat in Lurch I reviewed everything in my mind that I would now never experience again. Lysol. The wet streets. I wished I could be in those wet streets now. The rising and tightening vortex of a rose's labia. The salt smell licking off the ocean. My self-deception. The classroom. Too late. They had gone home. Why was I still here? I couldn't fit the pieces together.

"I have a class right now. I have to go."

"You had a class, but it's over. Those students are gone. You'd be sitting in your office now."

"You don't know anything about my office."

"I know about your office. It's Room 43A. I know you're a philosophy professor. I know you're doing shit."

"What shit? What do you know? Tell me right now." My voice cracked, but he didn't hear me because a car horn banged and drowned me out.

"Nobody is even going to notice you weren't there today."

"I was sick."

"You don't look sick."

The room was streaking and bending.

"I do feel sick." My voice felt around in the dark like a blind person.

"Well, nobody would believe that. I think we should go now."

"People will be looking for me."

"Nobody knows you're here. It's not where your type of people hang out."

What did he mean by that? Who were my type of people? I didn't want to ask questions. Sitting here with him was a mistake. Nothing else could happen.

"You'd never come here. Except to look for me and now you've found me."

I felt hot. I was going to cry. But I couldn't cry.

"Get up now and follow me out."

I am an analytic philosopher. It is my job to calibrate risk. The bartender still hadn't come back. Bobby, Bobby. Where was Bobby? Saying the name in my head soothed me like something Pastor Kevin would have said. Bobby, Bobby, let us all rejoice in his name. He will take us to the Kingdom of Ends.

I hadn't paid my bill. But Bobby would come back. This wasn't the eighties. The economy. Interest rates. Too dangerous to leave doors unlocked. He would call me a cab. I couldn't get to my car. It was two blocks away. Too drunk. An empty street. A broken abandoned building. A lot with a chain link fence and a Do Not Trespass sign. They'd read about it in the paper. What was Hanks doing? Online dating? One year earlier a girl's body was found near the rose bushes. The police had the area taped off. But the public was hungry for information.

"What are all the police doing there, Mommy? What are they digging for?"

"Nothing!" A woman yanked the child away. "Buried treasure."

We all heard about the girl on the news the next day. People left flowers. Carnations. Roses. Petals withered and fell and people stepped on them with their shoes. Candles shivered in little tin cups. And that would be the punch line to my life.

Drunk. I didn't drive recklessly. Was not a rule breaker. Walk away! What would they think? What was wrong with me? The room still tilting.

You don't deserve your job. Nobody would get into this situation. Not Denke. Blegg. Or that moron LeBec. Based on this situation alone, LeBec deserved my position. There was a reality show in that: *Stupid Fucking Cunts*.

My voice strangled in my throat as the room dissolved away. I reached my hand down to push myself up again. He caught my wrist. His eyes looked like two dark TV screens. I could see my reflection. But nothing else. No feeling or emotion moved in those black holes. The light from above glinted full in his eyes.

"You're a sign," he whispered.

I pushed myself up again.

Then he said, "I knew you were going to do that."

Bobby. Bobby. Where was Bobby?

"Let's go. What are we waiting for?"

A car hissed by in the rain. Then another.

The smell of Lysol pitched high in my nostrils again. Go outside. Run. Someone would stop. They'd see a woman running. If I could get home everything would be all right. The street had been crowded on my way into Lurch. He wouldn't hurt me there. I would stop the police or a bus or a cab. Everything would be okay.

"I'm going," I thrust my voice at him. "Alone."

He didn't say anything, but stood when I stood. He was tall. Built. Caged me with his body. He could kill me in a second. I pushed the door open. He limped out behind me to the street. I walked out the door, and he followed me.

The wind blew silver needles of rain. I burst ahead. Ran. Then looked back. His shot leg twisted, stuck out at an angle as he clutched the sleeping bag and began to shuffle behind me through the wet shadows.

The car turned down the road. It curled alongside the path. I stopped and waved wildly to get its attention. The car sped up then disappeared behind the black strip of the horizon, its high beams cutting across my face.

"Look at you. Just look at you," my mother would've said. "What do you expect when you don't wear lipstick or a pair of heels. You look like a dead person."

The high-contrast lipstick and pale skin.

A look that could take you straight from morgue to open casket.

I didn't care what she thought. It made me want to keep

wearing what I've always worn, the black square heels. Black, black, and more black

"Now, that's a look."

I bristled with a dark joy thinking how I'd managed to elicit her disapproval.

"I'm not trying to impress anyone."

"At least that's something we can agree on."

I ran down the street, glancing back to see his shards catch and flash in the light of the streetlamps and the moon. He didn't have a chance and fell far back, disappeared behind me just as the car disappeared ahead.

I turned a sharp corner, then pushed through a hole in the bush and scrub that led down to the water and my apartment about a mile away.

In the black sky, the barely visible crows circled and shrieked above my head, their eyes and beaks flashed and changed. My feet splashed in puddles soaking into my shoes and the moon as it quivered and shook along the path. The trees, the path, the lights on the distant water.

You know what you did!

It didn't mean anything. I glanced back.

He'd grown smaller.

Just a glint of a speck.

Out of the side of my eye, the lights of a car flashed. I hadn't even noticed it watching and glowing, waiting behind the hedge.

The two white circles blazed, floating toward me.

I turned and cut through the tall grasses beyond the path, my legs and arms cutting through the growth all the way down the slope to my apartment.

At the top of my stairs I stopped, panting, turning back to

put my hand on my door. He clutched the wet sleeping bag, sopping and heavy as the rain streamed down his face.

"What the fuck? How did you get here?" Then I noticed under the sleeping bag, a skateboard tucked under his arm. "I thought your foot was hurt."

His body braced behind me through the door to my apartment. The glare of the car made it too bright to see as it crawled toward us.

He grunted, pressing his weight against me. "Open it."

The car lights flashed.

"Open the fucking door." His mouth burned into my skin.

"I'll call the police." I unlocked the door. He slid in fast.

He banged the elevator button open, pushing behind me until we reached my apartment and my keys clicked the door open.

He sidled up to the window. Lifted the curtain. Peered out. Then dropped it. "Get down," he hissed, pushing at me with his hand. I crouched below the window then fell to the floor. He dropped from the window, flattening himself back against the wall. Reached over. Pulled the string to shut the curtain.

He motioned for me to get up. Shivered past the marble side table, disappearing into the bathroom. I stared at the bathroom door. A little slit of light ran back and forth along the bottom of the door. It trembled then broke.

He reappeared, clutching the orange sleeping bag soaked with rain, darkened and small like the pointed tips of the mountains outside the window.

"Who was in that car?" I asked him.

His eyes glinted past me fast in the dark.

"You have to go now. I'll call the police. I will call them."

He still just stood there.

The phone rang. I picked up.

A woman's voice barked, "I know he's there. Let me talk to him."

"She wants to speak with you."

"Tell her I'm not here," he gasped, clutching his bad leg.

"Is she out there in that car? How did she get this number?"

"Tell that bitch I'm not here," he said again, sidling up next to me.

"Who are you looking for?" I asked the voice.

"Just put him on."

"I'm alone."

"No, you're not," she snapped.

I held the receiver out to him. He stood there.

"I'm alone," I repeated and hung up the phone. I turned to him, "What are you getting me involved in?" I said. "I'm sure there is someone who can help you. Covenant House or some government agency."

He paced in front of the window. Then reached down and pulled off the hoodie. He wore just a T-shirt. He was tall, lean, well defined. Larger iterations of the thin blue vein in his jaw pulsed under the skin of his arms.

"Haven," I said, almost shouting it. "I can no longer offer it. I can't help you," I told him. "I've been fair and reasonable. I've listened."

Go, I screamed inside my head. Move in some direction. But my throat tightened. My eyes flicked toward the door. So did his. He held my eyes. I flinched forward. He didn't move. I lunged toward the door. He turned quickly and blocked my way. He was taller than me. I didn't want to look up.

I felt the dark gap. His wet hair. His eyes. I saw myself inside them. The empty black glass. Broken TV sets. If I moved again, even an inch, something would happen.

He was going to strangle me. In less than a minute, I would be dead. He'd use the hoodie to clean the blood then he'd wrap me in the sleeping bag.

"Go!" I said. "Please just go."

"Nobody's going anywhere," he said. "You think I'm playing. Who do you think I am? I'm here. I'm standing right here. This is what you wanted, right? Check it out." He turned his wrist to me fast. I thought I saw my name, Del, inside a heart.

I meant to take his wrist, just to be sure of what I thought I saw, but he was standing at an angle, so I had to pull his arms to me. When I touched him, I could feel the veins, ropey and wild, as his eyes narrowed sharply behind that hair. It was so strange how fucking hot he was. I was one hundred and fifty percent certain I'd never been this close to a guy this hot even in my dreams and without even a beat and before I could even neurologically process what was actually happening I felt myself sliding away, almost separating from my rational self, so that my rational self didn't even exist anymore, as I ran my hands along his arms to his shoulders. He grabbed me hard, nose and mouth deepening into me. Kissing me. He didn't smell bad, but musky and sweaty like B.O. before it turns and some smell that was like some fading combination of weed and patchouli. My shitty boring life seemed so far away now. I felt like I was sixteen, and I suddenly felt like I was having the life I would have had if I'd been born someone else and that other life seeped in and filled up those spaces inside me. I didn't want it to slip away just as I slipped deeper inside him. I wanted to keep this thing forever like a key on a charm bracelet. I pulled back. He looked up, still peering at me between those triangles, his eyes and lips heavy.

"Wait! Tell me your name."

"Don't ask me that shit." He whispered into my skin. "You know this is different." Did I know that? I didn't even catch my breath to ask him what he meant by that before he pressed himself against me. His lips. His hands. Tightened until only the dark breathed between us. The other tattoos. Numbers. Cat. Thunderbolt. Dollar sign. Heart. Blue bruises. Red. Words I couldn't make out. I touched the bones of his wrist. The Del inside the heart. Crushing me down onto the couch as if he were trying to scrub something off onto me. Pressed down, tightening between us. The moon made parts of him glow. Was there a leak in the ceiling? I touched his face. He jerked it to the side. My shirt. His lips. His eyes. My eyes. Everything. Burning. Burning away. He flashed against me from above with the moon, his hair shivered small slivers of broken glass.

WHEN IT WAS over, he withdrew into his corner, pulling on his pants. His voice far away, talking to himself. "It's funny. The first time you do something it stays with you, but you don't know it until later. All you can do is write a song about it."

He pulled the hoodie over his head. It swallowed him up. He looked smaller than I'd remembered. His chest curved inward like something we'd done had made it collapse. His hips, knees, elbows stuck out at sharp angles. The stubble on his cheek looked like dirt. A tiny fear sucked inside me.

"What do you mean? How old are you?"

He was pulling on his socks. Stuffing his feet back into his shoes. "Seventeen."

"No, you're not. Don't be stupid," I said, checking his face, but his expression didn't change. An intense white heat flashed inside me. "What? Are you joking?" The words lashed out. "Is that a joke?" I asked him. Then I said, "If anyone asks me about this, I'll fucking deny it."

I somehow walked myself over to the window after he left and yanked open the curtains. I stared at myself in the black pane of glass. Just as I had thought when he was still standing here, I knew at some point he would be gone and I'd try to memorize all the little details. Later, in the bathroom, I splashed my face with water. The towel clung and bunched to the rack.

The next morning, fear and self-loathing paralyzed me. I made my way into the rainy and dark morning streets.

As soon as I saw it, that dark hole of a stairwell crystallized my sense of stupidity and incompetence. No longer did I feel the excitement and joy of stepping into the black rain. I watched for him down the hall and the tremble of light under the stairwell.

Before my class, I crouched under the stairwell. Stared into its mouth. The pimpled concrete walls. The undersides of the stairs painted over by a routine maintenance job. No smells permeated from the dwelling.

I stood behind the lectern. The students packed in their tight rows along the graduated floor: Cassidy and Mike, the prize students, the pair I intended to recommend for the Honours, and all the others not as brilliant, but well intentioned, especially that hideous Mary Ann: pink, truncated, ran around doing all the photocopying. I stumbled over my notes as faces, words, thoughts stuck together as thoughts of him, his face, his eyes, his dream, his unknown female caller blurred together.

Afterward, as the students shrunk away, a layer of ice grew and separated me from this world as I grew afraid that someone could tell.

LeBec passed me in the hallway, smiling that same tight smile, cooing that mawkish, "Good morning, Del," voice tinking as she drew out my name again.

No one would find out. No one ever could find out.

Then it struck me that I didn't even know his name. No matter how hard I looked under the stairwell, no tremble of light.

Rape.

The word bleated in my head. Yes, that was what I would tell them.

Someone had been raped.

But it wasn't me.

I took the long way home, driving past Lurch, the forest of the park, too terrified to get out of my car, searching everywhere for him, for any hint of him, for the glint of his eyes, or even just the slightest orange flicker from that dog of a sleeping bag.

III

I MADE EVERY EFFORT to pull myself together for the next few days and weeks after the night it happened right through to Christmas—a holiday I didn't participate in or acknowledge: I did not want to be sucked into the rampant excesses of late capitalism as it forged its mighty inroads into fascism. In my day, you were lucky if you got a pair of socks and an orange. Now the stores were bursting with plastic toys that deteriorated in children's bedrooms while their pink lungs pumped. The university kept moving along. Committees, new faculty hires, tenure, promotion, like an animal feeding itself just to stay alive. I attended to academic responsibilities, even sitting in my office alone during the holidays, walking swiftly through the tunnel to check the stairwell for any sign of him glinting in that black hole while I suffered through my manuscript.

I was glad to escape my apartment. Krevice, my landlady, was always sweeping out the lobby. Wore tamped-down slippers made of terry towel. Corrugated nails grew out of thick yellow nubs. For the past few months, Krevice had knocked on my door with noise complaints.

"I'm not naming names," she would say.

Her eyes fixed on something in the distance as if I repulsed her. The neighbours spied on me. Stared at me with suspicion. Wrote threatening letters. Tetrault on the right, bony skull pressed against my wall. Silverstein below, face screwed up in distrust. He walked the building in backless leather slippers and pajamas, cracking a rolled newspaper against his leg, hissing, "Terrorist." Upstairs a nameless girl with fat pink cheeks grinned moronically at the panel of elevator buttons. Her mattress springs squeaked as she screamed profanities. What right did they have to lodge a noise complaint?

An ideal occupant, clean, nonsmoker, quietly industrious. I paid rent. Me, the single, older woman, vilified, treated like a stranger, misfit, castaway, or prostitute.

The day after the night of the stairwell guy, Krevice slid an envelope under my door, containing another complaint, typed and signed with a pen. Nobody used a typewriter anymore. I examined the perforations the hammers made into the paper.

I DECIDED NOT to postpone tenure. I couldn't risk Denke's disapproval, but wondered if our conversation had thrown off his support of my file. The committee would soon meet. Whenever my anticipation escalated, a sliver scratched to the surface.

The sign down the hall said *Pisado Majado*: Wet Floor. Followed by a translation in several other languages whose characters I didn't recognize.

Do not slip. Do not make a mistake.

"If you make a mistake," John McGilvery would've said, "make it interesting."

"What's interesting?"

"You know, rape. Murder."

A few nights later, the phone stunned me out of bed long past my ten p.m. curfew. Nudging my feet into plaid slippers, I picked up the receiver.

"Let me speak to Cody," demanded a voice. A woman's voice. Dark, throaty. The voice from before. His girl. "Please, put Cody on the phone."

The voice halted, breathless, a movie star trying to sound like a little girl, but taking on the hard grating edge of someone tweaking on meth.

"Who is this?" I asked.

A sound muffled and the line broke. I held the receiver. Cold, hard.

Two minutes later, it rang again.

"I need to talk to him." The voice frayed in my ears, "Cody!"

"You have the wrong number," I told her. "I don't know a Cody." I depressed the button, laying the telephone on its cradle.

The next day, again, the phone rang. Despite myself, I picked up. "Look, if you know where he is, tell me now." Her voice softened, "I'm begging you. Put Cody on the phone. I need to talk to him."

"I'm sorry," I said.

Her voice quickened. "Don't hang up. Please. Tell him I love him." I did hang up. Her voice had a distressed quality. Thin, cheap material sewn by children in a foreign factory. Disturbed. A child herself. A child with a phone and a car.

She called a few more times. Urgent, desperate, whining. I smothered those rings with a pillow until they stopped. But I didn't want to turn off the ringer. I couldn't help thinking about the alleged Cody. This girl. That little shit must have given her my number. How much did she know about me? What could she do? Was it her in the car that night? Cody himself missing. Unpredictable. Dangerous. But eventually, the phone, smothered by the pillow, did stop ringing. I still couldn't concentrate on my research. The completion of the manuscript, the course preparation. Yet even through December as the

Christmas tchotchkes sparked the sky, nothing dulled the points of my fear.

On the eve of January, as the New Year's revelers lit the streets on fire, I flashed awake. He knew where I lived. Where I worked. My office. He could jeopardize tenure. Or slash my throat. A ruby necklace. Not to be confused with a pearl necklace.

"Well, at least he gave her something before he left," they'd say at my funeral. "Talk about a cheap gift!"

"Give me the pearls over rubies any day."

The public shaming. My colleagues would be summoned to a meeting, staring with rapacious curiosity while Denke unfolded the news, flattening it out on the table like a map. Their stunned faces. Tanis permanently lodged in hospital. Her crushed eyes. Denke's bleak furrows, concealing the unspeakable. LeBec's juicy delight.

THE NEXT WEEK I delivered my first lecture of the New Year on my esteemed mentor's *The Five Pointed Star*, in which all five ethical theories glistened from each point and extended outward, forever moving and changing.

"How is it possible that every theory can reach the same conclusion?" asked a pair of blinking blank eyes.

"Read the syllabus. You can go back to Heidegger and, before him, Heraclitus," I said. "The world is always changing like the five fingers of a star."

I waved my fingers.

The way McGilvery became so devoted to teaching his students to think in terms of absolute principles of morality, principles that could then be acknowledged, discounted, and discarded would equip everyone to be a better person in a better world. In the same way he'd said to me, "Christ, Del, nobody died."

The students had lined up to get a glimpse as he lectured. The blue smoke blossomed, making the world look more exceptional than it really was.

If McGilvery's first book drew together all theories of moral philosophy, his second, *The Five Pointed Star*, would prove that by investigating each razor sharp point of these theories, one could then discard them one by one to fully understand that there is no single moral truth.

Decades earlier, when my mentor had sat there on the throne of his office chair, he considered himself more a scientist on the verge of a medical discovery than an academic fulfilling a publication quota. As he told *Time*, "I have devoted my life to proving that a moral truth is a false notion." When asked if his work was post-apocalyptic, he said, "Look around you. This is the apocalypse."

He would insert similar comments as he dictated steadily and flatly to me about ethics, further developing his theory of the five pointed star. I couldn't help wondering what would happen to his wife, Susan. Nevertheless, the brazen genius would continue dictating, "We must return to Heraclitus and his view on reality's constant flux. We cannot throw out Kant's imperatives. Our being constantly changes, and yet we require the constancy of rules. In this paradox, we have the flash of a star. Each of its five points represents a different ethical theory that until now were in stark disagreement, and we must reject the entire principle of one unifying moral truth."

He would move the five fingers of his hand. "Ethics, like life, moves and changes. Therefore, we must capture perception, fleeting and fast, and the way the eye holds it all together to create symbols. We need to make sense of our lives. Otherwise, we can't recognize true moral value should we discover it in some dark wet patch."

At this point, McGilvery and I were having sex every day. He'd lock the door of his office, brushing up against me as I typed. Then he'd lean me over his desk. "It's an old academic trick," he'd whisper. "If I turn off the lights, nobody will know we're here." Carved into the back of his desk, the word fucker popped and burst with each thrust.

He singled me out. I wanted to say the right thing. To intrigue him.

But first he saw me. Waited. Then, "What are you doing here?"

"I dunno."

"Well, come in, damn it. Don't just—"

I would hand him the stack of notes just as he opened the door for me to come in, grumbling, kicking out some student, then pulling the door closed behind us, dictating, his voice as sharp as the five points of his star.

I used my hand to look for the blood.

He sat at The Nook—solicitous, magnanimous, nothing to lose. Shimmering. A dream. Yes, he was my professor. Yes, to the year. 1987! Leather boots. The Kit Kat Club. The Pyramid. Neon strips of colour moving so fast past the corners of your eyes were actually flawlessly beautiful women.

Yes, he picked me. Gazed at me. Handsome. Dark. He looked at me like I was the girl in an ad, an ad for skin-tight jeans worn by a girl turning into a woman at the very moment the photo was shot. Was this really happening? He was my professor.

"I hate this." He'd hold his head in his hands. "You don't understand. This is shit. What is this place, this so-called Ivy League bullshit? This is nothing."

I wanted to ask him why he didn't go somewhere else.

I didn't dare ask him that.

Everything under forty is the end of the beginning. Everything over forty is the beginning of the end. Twenty years ago, I was at the beginning of the beginning.

Then he laughed at me. The back of his throat clucked. Not sharp or derisive. The way he laughed at the other philosophers and members of faculty. He treated me like a confidante, an equal. I was secretly thrilled, didn't allow my face to betray me.

"Do you even understand how fucked this is?" Then softly, not dismissively, almost as if something in my face had convinced him. "You do, don't you?"

He never asked me personal questions. So as not to intrude or invade.

"Another poor little rich girl. Another princess."

Let him believe I'm like those other girls, I thought, as he backed me up against the edge of the desk.

Time stretched to a point of absurd surrealism. Perpetual euphoria. Movies. Big wet mouths. Late night television. Under my acrylic afghan. Ice cream out of a carton with a spoon. Made me to want to scream so hard. Yes! Yes! Yes! I pressed my fist to my mouth as my life drained down a dark hole. Yes, I said to no matter what—even if it hurt. Because even when it did hurt, it still felt so good.

Squeezing me slowly out my own hole until there was nothing left inside, nothing more than a vague impression of a young woman at college everywhere I went.

EVEN WITH MY training, my mental rigour, I couldn't disentangle the alleged Cody from my thoughts. I told no one. Had Tanis not been decomposing in a hospital, I would have unloaded the whole mess onto her front lawn. But at that point we each had our own nightmare to contend with. I envied hers, one that would've made sense and elicited the sympathy of my peers.

The first time I visited Tanis in the hospital she was still undergoing treatment. Frenzied activity strobed the halls as medical staff hurried back and forth.

The providence of science!

Take your doctor's hand. Put your faith in them.

Patients were propped up in gurneys as their families sat in chairs, happily chatting and drinking from paper cups.

A sign posted to the door read: No shoes, no cancer, no service.

Another read: Chemo patients, please double-flush toilets after use.

When I walked in, Tanis gave me a wan smile. She wore a green smock tied in the back. She was covered by a sheet and a thin white blanket. The white circles of the ceiling lights glared down on us just as the black circles around her eyes glared at me. She looked like a picture of someone who'd been beaten by their husband.

"Are they treating you okay?"

"It's great. We're having a sweet DJ tonight. You should come."

Her eyes were hard and shiny. She was smiling.

"I've had like a different doctor every day," she said. "It's like speed dating. It's amazing how nice people can be when they know they'll probably never see you again."

"I'm sure we'll laugh about this in fifty years," I said.

She was still smiling, but her eyes tightened. She was angry. Struggling. A child glaring at its mother.

I sloshed with shame and fear. It was a bad drink. Who knew what the hell else was in there? Just keep it together until you go. My eyes kept pulling away from her. I would've done anything to help her just to make that feeling go away.

"I forgot. I got you something." I pulled out a box of Rough Riders. Put it on the bedside table. "They were out of vanilla."

Her face twisted. Then it cracked, vibrated, and tears seeped between the cracks. "Fuck! Fuck! I didn't want to do this."

"Are you okay?" I didn't know what to say.

She glared at me as if everything I said made it worse. "What do you think?"

I didn't say anything. I wanted to change the subject and leave her with a joke, maybe. A good feeling. That should've been the goal of this visit, but it quickly turned into something else I didn't expect or want.

"I've got to get back. Denke is breathing down my neck about my citations. He actually thought I should take Helene for lunch. Like that's ever going to happen."

A sick feeling seeped inside me, but I couldn't stop.

Tanis honked into a wad of Kleenex. "I wouldn't worry about your citations."

"Of course, I'm worried. Anybody would be worried."

"I don't think *you* should be worried."

I would've taken what she'd said as a compliment, a vote of confidence, but she darkened and twisted as if she'd said something she shouldn't have. My heart accelerated. I wanted to run away and cry, but then I wouldn't find out what she'd meant. "Do you know something?"

"What do you mean?" she said, wiping her nose.

"You said not to worry about the citations. What did that mean?"

She looked angry. "Nothing."

"I won't say anything."

"No, Del, I don't know anything." The words came out hard and fast as if she'd fired them out of a gun muzzle. I waited for her to soften, but she gave me a punitive glare. I was afraid to move. Scared I'd miss some important sign, symbol, or take away that could change my destiny. We both wanted something we couldn't get.

I muffled goodbye, rushing into the hall. Pushed past a cluster of doctors. Tanis called behind, "If I find out anything else about your tenure, I'll be sure to get in touch."

WAITING FOR WORD of my tenure, all I could do was trudge along with my lectures, hardly remembering the words as they came out of my mouth. The students stared ahead like agonized, frozen heads on sticks, so I assumed I had not managed to braid a rational line of inquiry. I spoke for forty minutes then waited until they'd gone.

"Look at you. Just look at you, tricking and faking them as usual," my mother would have said. "That's what I call a con job."

"I am an imposter. I guess I'll just have to reconcile that within myself."

"You've made your bid."

And every night the girl continued to call, hissing into the phone, "Don't hang up this phone. Don't you dare hang up this phone, and put him on. Put him on the phone."

An electric silence buzzed on the other end.

"You'd better put him on this phone right now, goddamn it," she cried out.

Fucking stupid whore bitch slut, I wanted to yell, but the following phrase bleated inside me repeatedly: This call may be recorded for quality and training purposes. I held the phone in my hand then carefully placed it on the cradle.

Based on his taste, I imagined she would be a younger version of myself—a heavy breather. A nail-biter. Dyed hair. Too much make up. Tight, cheap, plasticky smelling clothes. Ate treats in bed when no one was looking. Ding Dongs, Rob Boys, Chuckanuts. Barely moved, turning the steering wheel of her car with one hand while smoking cigarettes and digging into a bag of treats she kept hidden in her underwear drawer with a copy of the Holy Bible...smoked mentholated cigarettes. They'd met in an institutional setting. His counselor, neighbour, parole officer, nurse. Raccoon-ringed, slutty, wet, crying eyes. A rash of murder-eyed, dirty knives tucked in her pants, a driver's license. His hands all over her. Car. Sticky seats. Cigarette burns. Packages of chips crackling under their bodies as they rolled in sync to Poolboy. The stench rising. The sweat. Ejaculate. Cheap drugstore perfume. They'd separate, picking the coins off their skin. I searched Poolboy on the laptop. Skinny tattooed, urban thug, moved his hips suggestively to a low beat played on repeat as a dark taunting sensation slipped in and out of me.

"Come on, something's going on," said Blegg. She sidled up beside me in the cafeteria, melamine tray resting on her enormous belly. Voice lowered, conspiratorial. A smile almost as smug as LeBec's. "Is it a man?"

It was as if I had grown into a foreign species that had been grafted to another species and would soon be rejected by its host. I could not remember why and how I'd come here, where I was now. Even as an undergrad, I couldn't focus on anything but the shiny flat moon in the sky.

Back in university, I'd clenched with fear. Struggled with book after book. Each word dissolved into the next. "Analysis is the sorrow of the mind." I had no idea what I was doing there. The scholarship winner from Wilbur Smith. I missed the sheer mundane, moronic simplicity of Slaughter. I'd worked the cash register. Flipped magazine pages with dirty fingers. Dutch Maid chips. Coins. Canadian sugar pies from cellophane packages. Twinkies. Dutchies. Cream-filled logs indistinguishable from my own fingers. Bit my own thick white fingers.

McGilvery didn't eat. Created with his body a vehicle of crystalline moral purity through which he passed those five pointed stars.

I'd slide my hand under the cash register where I kept my favourite issues of the magazines, the ones featuring the celebrity mothers on the cover. Where true love coalesced into something unquestionable and unbreakable. The pregnant movie star stood there with her man on her arm looking as pleased as a big game hunter who had just stalked and killed her prey.

I smeared the pages of *Us, People, Star.* Powdered sugar. Love, sex, motherhood rolled into giant red mouths, glistening teeth, white, delirious, triumphant.

Keep your smile Ultra Brite!

Diamonds are his duty and your prerogative!

Animals are made to be seen—on you!

From the dirty yellow light high above, celebrity mothers winked.

"They've got to love you if you have their baby."

"You can't take that off after a fight and throw it out the window."

"The gift that keeps on giving."

"He calls it child support. But I call it a Porsche 911."

Squeezed under the acrylic blanket. A mini TV. The carton of ice cream perched on my stomach sweated. Softened. Rotated the antennae until they broke off in my hands.

"John McGilvery," said *Time*, "will guide us toward a better humanity."

He'd laughed sharply. With his hands, spread the door wide open. Spilled light out. Thrust me inside that urgent box and closed the door until the word fucker popped and burst.

Our Philosophy parties. Up and down halls. My paper plate. Tiny circles, squares, the crackers, the cheese. Hands vibrated. Stood off to the side. Not like those girls with their perfume—Charlie or Halston, or Love's Baby Soft—as freshly powdered as a disposable diaper, eyes spanked wide open, blinking with the sheer bewilderment of being alive. Pressed against the walls. Voices husked. "Marlboro Lights?" Just like those sharp-eyed boys through the metal bars. Pressed against the counter at Slaughter. Passing the money at me through the cash slot in the security grille. Hands sliding against mine, moist as a secret. Gotcha! Looked past me through the window. That girl waited for them on the passenger side, staring ahead like a queen, exhaust blossoming around her.

Annie Money and her group interrogated each other with a tone. Hard. Blunt. Slapped into shock by their own stupidity.

"Aren't you on the pill?!"

"I wanted to meet Luca in Viareggio, but I won't have the money now."

"Ask your dad."

"You mean my dead, cause that's what he's going to be when I tell him I need an abortion. I mean, after he strokes out."

"And if he does stroke out, he won't even notice if you take his money."

"I know, right."

"That's actually stealing," I'd call out from behind my book.

Those Annie Moneys and those other girls. Watched them from the corner of my eye. Tangled on her bed. Whispered and colluded.

"Is she listening?!"

They'd sigh and groan with frustration.

"Why don't you keep the baby?" I said.

"God, Del, it's not a baby." They laughed.

"It's not like she's going to marry him."

"Don't listen, Del!"

"Fuck! God!"

The year before I left Wilbur Smith, a few of those Slaughter girls grew pregnant. Dropped out. Belonged to those boys now in a permanent way. Tiny tensile helixes chained them throughout the millennia with blood and lust.

MCGILVERY GAVE ME a hard look. A warning. Didn't want the others to know about us. "I'm a moral philosopher."

"We have to be careful."

"Don't give me that look in public."

"Don't stand so close."

I understood.

He didn't have to tell me twice.

Not like those other girls. He'd roll his eyes at them. They humiliated themselves, giggled, thrust at him with their long shiny hair and tiny hips. Confident in their natural beauty. Didn't need to wear makeup, backcomb, use hairspray or imitate the cheap leather girls on album covers.

Biographers would discuss how we sat in The Nook. Meetings. Secret. Flagrant. Took that chance. In public. What did we talk about? People might have speculated, as I often speculated. Even the cashier at The Nook with the scrunchie and the big teeth, wondered, *Why her?* as she rang in our coffees with a nasty look.

Men take time to mature and find out what they want. Always the last wife reaps the rewards of that paradigm, they would say as a silver bead shivered up my spine.

The way McGilvery looked at me in The Nook twenty years ago as if it was the last time he was going to see me, memorizing my face.

"Please," he rasped, "stand over there."

He had a wife.

Susan.

His biographers would say he and Susan were still married. As much as he didn't love her, he also didn't hate her. They'd consider our relationship in a series of fast forwards. They'd say he finally found what he needed from the back row.

Baffled by everything except those movie magazines at Slaughter.

Slaughter, Slaughter, so far away, so I didn't think. My brain trembled. My eyes. The stars. I didn't know what to do.

AFTER OUR TALK about withdrawing my application for early tenure, Denke had stopped looking in on me. He lingered in the hall. LeBec nudged up beside him. Whispered strained, codified words. Pops, hushes, squeaks ratcheted deep in the throat. I didn't understand. I must have missed the email announcement of this new delivery system.

After the Beeby Prize and the Mahon dinner, LeBec had ignored me, no longer stopping me in the halls to coo about this or that scholarly or departmental news.

Now Denke didn't return calls, emails. He'd stopped asking about the book. I sensed a shift. My colleagues passed me in the halls with a sharp angularity as if I incubated a contagion, intentionally left me off the email and Twitter feeds that advised they avoid me. Maybe they could detect my transgressions. Soon to be the subject of academic lore and ridicule.

I, too, was not immune to LeBec's manipulations, flattered by this shining academic who once complimented me and now looked at me with loathing and disgust.

Then two weeks into the second term, I looked up to see LeBec dawdling at my office door. "Del, do you have a sec?" Before I could answer she'd slumped in my chair. Threw her bags at my feet. Chewed on her lip ring. After a while she said, "This isn't me, you know."

I hated obfuscation, so I had to ask, "What isn't you?"

The indelible delineation between the tenure track and untenured faculty. I felt exhilarated that she came to me, and that she had problems of her own. There she sat, reduced and humbled. Her eyes lowered. Apparently I intimidated her. Her voice trembled. "Office politics. Do you know what I mean?"

I felt sorry for her.

Pastor Kevin.

Make provisions for the idiotic.

For they do not know the way.

"I know what you mean," I said.

"Jenks said I wasn't a member of faculty."

"Adjuncts are faculty."

"She doesn't take me seriously. She's an elitist."

Her characterization of Donna Jenks was accurate. A smile slipped out of my mouth's tight grip. "Jenks can be a little bristly."

"She hates me."

"I think you're being dramatic," I cautioned.

"Really?" Her voice lilted like a schoolgirl's. "Do you think so?"

"Nobody has time to hate anyone. You need to grow a thicker skin."

"I feel like such a dork for wasting your time."

"You're not a dork," I told her, standing up.

Then something happened. LeBec leaped up, pressed her chest against my arm as tight as a child hugging a tree trunk. Her heart quickened one, then two beats.

I did nothing to solicit or provoke this action. Day after day, she would return, closing the door, sitting in my chair. Complaining about one colleague or another, or as she put it, the "weak links" in our faculty. Each time, before she left, she would cling to me. I allowed her that single striking transgression.

No matter what they might say about me, I am not a machine.

LeBec came by my office every day for a week. At the end of that week, on the twenty-first of January, I'd defended one of our colleagues to her with what I'd perceived as a rather innocuous statement, "I don't think that Hardy is slacker." LeBec stopped. A shadow crossed over her face. She abruptly stood up and left. No hug. No goodbye. Not a word. I stood in my office, blistering with confusion, deliberating whether to run after her. What horrible mistake had I made? Maybe it was my tone or that I'd disagreed with her. I obsessed about this for days, didn't see LeBec in the halls of our department or even in the library or the Philosophy student lounge.

A week later I waded through the green lawns while the rain and the wind moved the branches semaphorically. I neared the hem of the woods. My cell phone rang. Kalli ordered me to return immediately. An emergency meeting waited for me as fears about the boy, McGilvery, and LeBec tightened inside me.

I made my way back through the grass and the rain, castigating myself as I walked. Wondered if my colleagues might be sitting there around our department table to drop the sharp axe of their discoveries about my activities and put me out of my misery.

When I arrived, Denke announced that Jon Burns was now being dismissed. Burns, the colour of dishwater in an old white enamel sink, wore plaid shirts, face crowned with mousy blond hair, curling nerdily behind dated wire frames. Burns was not present at this meeting, but his book was. *The Amoralists* sat in the centre of the table like a rejected child about to be re-homed. The book had gained no traction. Had not met our department's research expectations.

As Denke put it, with LeBec beaming at him from across the table, Burns' position had to be put to a vote. Staring at my colleagues' blank, exhausted faces, my brain stretched back to that first faculty meeting when I'd overheard LeBec whispering to Denke that Burns' publisher was not a legitimate academic press. Streamline was perfectly respectable. As we all voted Burns out, LeBec's smile haunted me.

Since our disagreement, LeBec no longer stopped me in the halls. She had never invited me to join her group at the long pioneer table at La Range. Nor those drinks at the Garotte, and now she never would. Yes, I'd heard them talk about those nights shared by all but me. Their private words and snickers cut me as I passed by, their eyes hardening against me with fear and hostility. What a group of assholes. I decided I didn't care anymore. I had to decide that, after crying myself to sleep at night, I had nobody on my team. Nobody at all. I couldn't approach Denke, or Tanis in her hospital bed, or even Kalli. Kalli asked too many questions. Needed to be kept in the loop and invited to every party for her piece of cake. Imagine never being in the loop, Kalli! Ever!

Kalli took any question as an affront and a threat, massaged it for days. Maybe she was onto something: the sharp survival of the non-tenured staff.

I picked up the phone. "Have you seen Denke?"

"You keep asking me that. Wait. I think I did see him earlier. Hang on. There's nothing on his calendar." Then she said quickly, "Why do you need to know?"

Her tone had grown unusually officious, guarded, and flinty. Even suspicious. Kalli was usually more cordial with me, even friendly. But now she was cold. A jerk. She was terrible at this game. Didn't have the nuance to pull it off. I suspected that she'd been instructed to isolate me from Denke. She was his moat. A human fortification. I'd never get past her.

My job was now, officially, contaminated.

I had to take matters into my own hands. I flipped open my laptop. Even though I had no evidence to prove it, I somehow knew LeBec was at the bottom of all this. But LeBec was some kind of unparalleled academic rock star and I would never even come close to touching the fringes of her world, the world she infused with her brilliance. My ego couldn't tolerate even dipping a toe in that water. But that night, and for many nights after that one, I finally did what I dreaded most since I'd first met LeBec. I lost hours cyber-stalking her, scouring the internet. According to *Wikipedia*, both parents were academics. The mother a post-structuralist sociologist, only one species removed from philosophy, the father a biologist. The same college in Idaho. That scholarly pedigree, early grooming, black and white mobiles stimulate the fusing of cerebral continents.

Our discrepancies burned whitely.

My derelict upbringing. My dearth of intellectual stimulation. The girth of *People* magazines, candies, and colas hoarded in my underwear drawer.

My colleagues would give me points for exceeding expectations. If they knew!

Don't feed their prurient curiosity.

Don't bathe in self-pity. Tick down your list of world suffering—wars, starvation, the Holocaust, the Titanic's black, brackish water.

Then I scoured her Twitter feed. The rest of her social media brand. She had seven hundred and fifty-seven thousand followers. She had a hundred thousand likes. How was that even possible? The numbers pulsed inside me like an infection. It was travelling up to my heart and without the proper medical intervention would soon kill me. I could feel my organs shutting down. Systemic failure just around the corner. I began to pick through my stockpile before I returned to my laptop. What was the proper medical intervention? Clonazepam or Propanolol?

·LeBec was cycling and recycling tweeters and re-tweeters. Famous people. A writer who won the Pulitzer and allegedly molested a bunch of his students, a social activist drummer from a super hot indie band where all the guys had the same name and were super cute and dressed like little nerd girls, and even a famous award-winning journalist who tweeted, "Thank God for your tweets, Helene! A reason to get up!" What was that? Who needed tweets to get up? Was LeBec the new coffee and cigarette? Essential first thing in the morning and right before sleep even if we burned to death in our beds. I obsessed over each comment. Where did she have the time to pop off such little ditties as, "Our culture of meat has turned animal rights into animal rites." Or this one, "The supermarket is just another word for cemetery. Just as the zoo is code for soft-core zoophilia." She turned philosophy into a memoir, hashing genres like a mad genius working in her lab. Her website moved constantly like a rock video with dead animals, blood, chains transposed with images of crucifixions and even LeBec herself posed like a Madonna holding a lamb. Every image made me gasp. What the hell was going on? How was this academia? But it didn't matter anymore. Yes, the experience was crushing. I couldn't stop mentally juxtaposing LeBec's rock video against the wan photograph of me on our faculty website followed by my mundane biography. But after a while, once I submerged myself fully into the water, I became surprisingly okay with it. I even began to relish it in a BDSM kind of way. Then after a while I couldn't stop. It became a compulsion I returned to every night and what I thought about throughout the day. After a session of scouring the net, I'd feel horrible about myself, call myself a stupid cunt, then masturbate until I came. Yes, there were images of LeBec with Inu at Cannes premieres, at the Grammys standing with two rock stars Lil Douche and Pearl and Bob Smug (apparently up-and-comers, and they had their arms around her like they were all friends), a Marc Jacob's runway show at *New York Fashion Week* where she was positioned in the front row. There was even a photograph of her sitting on broken steps under the heat of a barrio with goats, but she was dressed like a little robot girl in a silver dress and giant platform shoes and calf-length green socks patterned with pink stars. Someone posted, OMG! She's so gorge. She looks like that singer Fidget. Then someone else posted, Yes, two gorgeous brainiacs. Who isn't jeal-ous! Then someone else posted, That's who I'd invite to my desert island. Then someone else posted, What desert island? I'm inviting them to the final dinner at my execution LOL! Her entire site was curated by the video artist, Imelda Bird, who had produced the hottest, edgiest rock videos (I had to look all this up) and was moving into feature films, but had still somehow had the time to design LeBec's site. Then the blog. Even that was genius, deep, visionary:

"It's funny how we'll do whatever we can to save the life of a parent or a child—even if we have no feeling toward them. Yet we have no qualms about sacrificing our pets if necessary or eating a steak without consideration for the kind and docile creature who witnesses friend after friend before them, or even a parent or sibling, disappear into the kill room until they, too, are led away to confront their own terrible fate. How have we as a species grown to view the meat stewing in our pot as a comfort smell?"

I don't know how she managed to create this coy narrative:

"Even as a child, I questioned the paradox at the heart of my meal. As I stared at my plate, I became stricken by moral conflict. What was the difference between this unnamed cow sacrificed for me and Pepperoni, our dachshund?

"In a sense, I could correlate this troubling domination and humiliation of another species with this meal, and my own desire to be controlled by D. This boy who carried me into the garage for my first sexual experience has become conflated with my later need to be restrained and humiliated. Now this unnamed cow that I have internalized has become part of that complicated narrative."

"A perfect hire. What a CV!" said Mahon.

"A slam dunk," said Denke.

"Did you hear Helene is travelling to New York, London, and Tokyo to promote her latest book?" Blegg felt compelled to tell me in the halls one day.

"I think it's just New York and London," I said. "Tokyo is postponed."

"No it's not," she said like I'd offended her.

It was as if LeBec was no longer her own person, but now belonged to all of us. And I was now our department's secret, official expert on LeBec. My obsession had taken on the hunger of a stalker, and I was sure my pathology was palpable to everyone. I couldn't stop, although the pain was excruciating as LeBec flashed back and forth through my head slowly, continuously, like the light on a photocopier. But it had become a good pain and the more I felt the burn, the more alive I felt.

She pervaded our cultural imagination. Her pedantic diatribes on the rights of the chicken and the mouse were compared to those of the world's greatest philosophers. She torqued her sexual perversions and imaginings. They didn't seem trite, but had weight, urgency, and relevance, and were discussed by intellectuals with the gravitas of the Holocaust and the Holodomor.

I took inventory of her accomplishments. My gut wrenched

repeatedly. A virtuoso. Selfies, showing off her shining, perfect face, so contrasted with my own flawed, pinched one. Her site pulsed, thrummed with streaming videos of LeBec, lectures, blog posts, the constant influx of comments, tweets, and even a link to an online talk she gave, perched on a stool, tiny baby voice, mini skirt, and grommets. I sucked all this in until I was numb with self-loathing.

The next day, flicking open my laptop, I received a strange alert: *Hi Del: Welcome to my site. How's it going?*

I slammed down the screen. Didn't even type a single letter in response. How did she track me? I didn't even know that was a thing. I forced myself to stop.

Now off brand.

I'd turned into a monster. Others must have suspected this potential in me.

Kept their distance as they wavered to the other side of the hall.

"People enter their fields for a reason," I had told Tanis at our very first lunch. "What's the difference between unethical ethicists and crazy psychologists."

"That's a little over simplistic, isn't it?"

I examined my colleagues one by one. Nothing good grew here. Nothing but stink, pollinators, ass kissers, liars, and backstabbers. The thing we aspired to, that once excited us, had died within us. LeBec was the sharp, alive thing we had all sacrificed within ourselves to get to this place of academia. Through her existence, she cut us until we bled out, staring at the banal reflections in our own red mucosa, but we still craved more of her. More of a reminder of what we weren't, but had once aspired to long before LeBec was even born. While we were still only children, putting ourselves to sleep with our own dreams and aspirations, she'd somehow sensed and incubated them, working on them even as her own DNA still lodged itself within her parents only to finally come together to spark, spin, and replicate. To ruin our lives. Even though I had embroidered my unfinished manuscript with my own narrative, I knew I could never even touch LeBec's work, her audacity and vision, without somehow now having my own called into question. She would now be our reference point, the gold standard. And maybe secretly all my colleagues felt the same way, they all had manuscripts that they turned to night after night to pour out their dirty little dreams, and once they discovered LeBec, maybe they too felt as though they couldn't finish their work, that they had wasted their lives.

By February, I was now terrified to return to my manuscript, even for a second. With so much at stake, my anxiety paralyzed me. I wondered if my argument was incoherent. I had concern for the consequences of actions. I couldn't reduce moral philosophy to a game, yet now I had a yawning sensation every time I worked on it as if my diastasis recti had split and the skin had thinned, thinned, thinned until it felt like it had burst open and parts of me were falling out. I needed to talk to someone about it, but there was no one I could trust except Tanis—seriously, my only friend left, and she was too sick. I couldn't tell whether *The Catastrophic Decision* was becoming a work of madness or genius or some half-baked pivot-point in between. The idea of writing a mediocre manuscript was the most horrifying consequence. After everything that had happened, I could hardly stand that. I had fantasies of destroying the manuscript. Setting it on fire. Time was of the essence. It had been weeks. I had to take stock. I fanned the pages out on the bed. Delicate, bone white, and perfect with the black etch of hieroglyphics. I was too vulnerable. Too filled with self-loathing. I knew immediately, it was a mistake to read it:

The Catastrophic Decision
Cont'd

I am still not treating another as a mere means. But I also don't want to treat myself as a mere means. Although, sometimes I would like to be treated as a mere means, but only with consent and a safe word.

According to the Kingdom of Ends, we are obligated to all rational beings. In a sense, even if other beings aren't rational, we are rational (a broad assumption) and are obligated to treat other creatures with the same respect and obligation as other rational beings.

Utilitarians view the character of experience not the subject of the experience.

In the calculation of utility, human interests outweigh the interests of the other non-rational beings also known as "others."

11A. If we calculate that the death of the other is better than the death of ourselves, primarily any other person, for whom is this death better? Surely not the other.

11B. Is the death of a human being worse than the death of a cat?

Answer: Ask the cat.

12A. Let's turn to Bully. I am ten years old. I live

next to a playground. There is a bully in the playground. One day I am playing with three kids in my
house. The bully comes to my house and knocks on
the door. The bully wants to kill me as well as the
three other kids. We are living in a post-apocalyptic
anarchist state. There are no police. I am an orphan.
The other three are also orphans. Do I allow the
bully into the house? The only weapon I have is a
pet hog. My furniture is all that prefab crap that
weighs five pounds, or maybe it's kid furniture. Little plastic chairs. I could drop a hog out of the
window to kill the bully and save the three kids. I
don't fully understand the consequences of drop-
ping the hog out the window. The hog could fall on
a bough or a horse and run away. The hog could
die. But my intention is not to kill the hog. What is
the moral consequence of pushing the hog through
the window?

12B. Maybe the hog will scare the bully away, but
maybe the hog's fall will be softened by the fall
onto the bully. Thus, would I be using the hog as a
mere means? Would the hog rationally choose to
jump on the bully?

Q: Why not use myself? A: I am not as big as
the hog. I am ten. I weigh 40 pounds and the hog
weighs 200 pounds. The bully is an estimated 80
pounds. Is there a way to morally justify using the
hog to make the bully go away?

We must parse our intentions. Should we kill the
one to save the three? Even if the one is a hog?
What if the one is a person? What if the one is two

persons? What if the person has the intelligence of a hog? At what point do we choose not to kill the one to save the three? What is the strongest moral position?

What if I built a contraption, a kind of ramp made out of my shitty prefab furniture, that allows the hog to walk to the window and jump onto the head of the bully? Would this be acceptable to all concerned? The hog may be encouraged, but not forced, to walk up the ramp. When the hog reaches the edge of the window, and the hog falls onto the head of the bully, would I then be using the hog as a mere means?

Note: As the hog would most likely agree, it is possible to have cake and to eat the cake just as it's possible to acknowledge the other and to eat them.

If it is morally acceptable to eat the hog, then why can't we use the hog to save the three? I would not eat the three, but I would eat the hog. Likewise, there is a very good chance the hog would eat me. But would the hog push me onto the ramp to save the three?

I cannot resolve these complex moral problems. You just need to find the legal loophole.

Subset 1: Insanity is a strong legal loophole.

Subset 2: Who isn't insane? Who couldn't argue that a person who eats their own family isn't some-how insane—*especially* if he knew what he was doing?

Exception: The Donner Family, e.g., one descendent held political office in California [probably because he had his whole family behind him.]

What is the relevant question?

13A. If the existence of the other threatens my own then would I not be justified in destroying the other to preserve myself?
Subset I: Is it rational to save our own life even if it means destroying the life of another?
13B. How do I make this moral decision?
13C. Can we make a decision based on self-interest?

Let's turn to Dress. Why can't I buy a dress from Fruman's? How much would it cost to buy a dress that could reasonably feed three hundred children? That would be $3,000 at ten cents a child per day. Some websites claim to feed a single child in some countries for three dollars per week. That means that one dress could feed one child for one thousand weeks. What kind of idiot would spend three thousand dollars on one dress? My dress cost one hundred and fifty dollars, which is only the equivalent of fifty weeks of food for that single child. Could we agree that everyone would rationally spend the money on the less expensive dress? What if I had nothing else to wear and everyone else wore an expensive dress? What if the three hundred starving children made the dress and got paid enough money to get food for the same amount of time it cost to make the dress? The dress I never wore.

As I continued to read, I became devastated. The book broke apart in my hands. My worst nightmare. The manuscript meandered. Made no sense. Moved with a funky, stiff walk as if a robot wrote it. But not an interesting, cool robot like LeBec. Just a hot robot like me (as in, not good hot, but as in hot mess), hot that technically blazed with mental illness if mental illness itself blazed with a white hot heat. Even I could tell the work was inconsistent, vacillating from brilliant to mediocre to less than mediocre and even to bad and, quite possibly, insane. My life was over, they would say. Finished. They would laugh at me. The final humiliation. I knew I couldn't tolerate it. *Fraud! Loser!* they would scream while covering me in honey and feathers. At this point, I had to confess, my goal was simply to not become a joke. I thought of LeBec's tiny smug smile. Denke's obsequious avuncular (and I mean the bad uncle) devotion to LeBec. I couldn't compete with it. I had nothing left. Was I at least a good person? After taking a quick inventory, I had to admit that I was, in fact, a shitty person, maybe even terrible. Maybe even worse. I wanted to see myself as someone who would not treat anyone—even Denke—as a mere means. Although, apparently, I was okay with myself being treated as a mere means. And although, if you look at my entire hideous narrative, maybe we were all used as a kind of mere means, really, when you got down to it. And I had to admit then that had I been drunk or stoned or even not completely freaked out, if I could just angle it in a certain way, *The Catastrophic Decision* might have looked brilliant again, but still I had to acknowledge that, in fact, I was naked, masturbating, and crying even now as I read it.

And now, as if to further push my face in this mud pie, which was in fact an adult version of a mud pie, which was a shit pie, and even after she'd tracked and caught me cyber-stalking her online, LeBec still wouldn't talk to me. Her eyes skimmed past me like I was a wall, and I nursed a dark, knifing betrayal. Cultivated fantasies of lashing out at her as if I were a child.

Then two weeks later on Valentine's Day, as people exchanged their tacky, disposable hearts, I sat in my office contemplating my fate.

I looked up to see LeBec framed in my doorway by a golden corona of light and dust, painted in that Byzantium tradition of tempura, egg yolk, gold leaf, ground pigments. The Theotokos of Vladimir. Exhilarated and confused. I had an impulse to drag out an endless stream of silky apologies as she closed the door behind her. Then, sitting in my chair, tilting toward me, she told me her plan to get rid of Gagne, a colleague, she perceived as a blight.

Blistering between rage and joy, I said, "That seems extreme."

She toed the strap of her bag with her boot, then seized my eyes, "He hasn't published in twenty years, Del!"

"I'm right behind him," I told her.

"You can't compare your research to Gagne's. Your work put us on the map internationally. It's like someone working on the cure for cancer."

"I think that's laudatory."

A tiny, primitive ball of anticipation turned in my mouth.

"I don't think it's laudatory," she said.

The next afternoon as I walked out of the elevator, I heard the phone ring from inside my suite. Twenty-four. And mounting. Twenty-six.

Listened to them one by one.

Nothing but hang-ups.

The phone rang again. I picked up. "Is he there?" Then she said, "Put Cody on the phone." Her voice strained, husked.

"Please. I need to talk to Cody. He doesn't have money. He won't eat. You have to make him eat."

"Is that code?"

"Don't fuck with me," she cried before I hung up.

The neighbours complained. Letters slipped under my door. Noise complaints because of the phone. Now the light flashed. Numbers escalated. Thirty-one. Thirty-two. Thirty-three. She didn't leave a message. Only hang-ups. I erased them one by one.

I dialed *69. Got nothing, but dead air and the message, "This number is no longer in service. Check your local listings."

I called the operator who said, "That number isn't listed."

"Well, I fucking well know that," I said.

"Did I answer the reason for your call?" she said.

I wanted to pull the phone out of the wall, but was scared if the woman couldn't call me, she might do something worse to get my attention. What she wasn't going to do was call the cops. But maybe she'd show up with her meth lab. Splash me with the same acid that burned the stairwell guy. Oh, you think that's a threat, I'd say to her. Boy, are you ever barking up the wrong tree. Do I look like someone who gives a shit about the way I look!? Or maybe she'd light the whole place on fire. Give the neighbours a real reason to complain and bitch. Write your letters now, you bastards!

The next day was no exception. The phone cried like a baby left alone in a department store. I crawled to it and picked up.

"I know about you. I've read your course outline."

"My syllabus?"

After I hung up, she kept calling that night and even later that week.

"I'm going to get you."

I didn't even breathe into the phone, hanging up each time before she had a chance to say anything more.

She called each night now. Hissed into the phone, "Don't hang up. Don't you dare hang up. I know he's there. Put him on."

I held the receiver in my hand. Then right in the middle of her words, laid it down on the cradle. Then one week after Valentine's Day the phone was already ringing even before I walked into the apartment. It rang, and rang, and kept on ringing. When I couldn't stand it anymore, I picked up.

"Don't believe anything he says. He's developed into quite a little liar. What has he told you? That you're beautiful? That you matter? You think I don't know? You think you can hide behind the walls of your bureaucracy? This isn't the 1970s anymore," she said. "The civilized intellectual with all her words and ideas, the Ivy League trained thinker, so far above us all. I'm going to get you. I know who to call. They'll come to your home and get Cody for me. And it's going to be gross. Do you know what I'm talking about?"

I hung up.

Did she mean gross? Or gross-gross? How gross are we talking here? Did she mean embarrassing gross or just a slight acid burn or limbs-off, balls-out gross?

The next day, Denke delivered the announcement of Gagne's dismissal. For a reason I can't explain, I was the first to thrust up my arm in support.

Peterson, tiny, pinkish, screwed as tight as a pig's tail, shouted out, "I condemn this atmosphere of bullying."

LeBec hesitated. Averted her eyes as if troubled by my brutality.

153

After a brief discussion, we were all dismissed. Gagne disappeared the next day. Apparently, he went on leave for a non-specific medical condition.

"What happened to Gagne?" I asked Blegg the next day in the hall.

"Apparently, he'd been sick for a long time," she whispered without stopping or moving her head.

Just as I had sat in front of the esteemed McGilvery at the meeting, our final, my smile so forced my cheek muscles ached.

"I thought you liked my paper."

"What paper? 'Analysis is the sorrow of the mind?' You didn't even write it. You didn't write a single word of anything."

"What do you mean?"

He'd rolled his eyes. "What do you want from me, Del?"

After I cried, he said again, "What on earth do you want from me? Christ, Del!" He said it as if he believed in Christ. "Nobody died."

LeBec came in and out of the offices of those she'd maligned in my own. Shared with them our same angled look, our same hug. Emerged even from Jenks' office. Eyes skirted mine without a trace of shame. Then strode away, striking the floor with her heels.

Opinions of LeBec escalated. My colleagues lauded her. Invited her to lunches and parties. I wanted to tear off LeBec's mask, but feared my colleagues would run away in horror and later hold it against me.

By late February, I did finally receive a group departmental email. Our colleague, Donna Jenks would be retiring at the end of the term.

At fifty-eight, Jenks' hair hung in a peppered curtain. She wore sandals teamed with wool socks. They explicated for her better than any social media site: Relate to me only through the world of the mind. I am no longer a sexual creature. Intercourse with me would be like wading through a sandbox.

The year before, Jenks had told us she couldn't afford to retire since she would need to support her elderly parents' transition into institutional life and beyond to that very final institution, the grave. I stared at the faces of my colleagues. Nobody questioned Jenks' retirement. I sensed that LeBec might beat and breathe behind it all.

IN EARLY MARCH, as the crocuses pushed their purple fists out of the ground, I had my first reprieve. Weeks before the end of term, the sky had finally cracked open. Black, starless. We had known the mountains existed, but hardly ever saw those frozen spikes. Now no longer objects of vast terror. Whole months had passed since that night the stairwell man/boy had forced his way into my apartment. The calls had dwindled. I was still terrified of the woman, but like many things in life, there are always some variables one can't control—like cancer risk or seismic issues. I just had to live with the amorphousness of life as Menzer had so often instructed. LeBec's contempt had turned to indifference. I had escaped. It was over. I had a job. An apartment. Tenure so close I could throw a stone and hit it.

Twenty years after everything that happened, this ostensible Cody wandered black streets, dragging an orange sleeping bag, sleeping in the forest or some deeply recessed doorway. But that night hadn't happened. That was my line, if they ever asked me. Just like that t-shirt I saw once, "If I can't remember it, maybe it *didn't* happen."

But it *did* happen. It actually happened. Evidence. Witnesses existed who could attest to the kid's very existence. I couldn't get out of this now.

I went to a philosophy seminar once on the legality of madness that argued that in time the term for insanity would be used to apply to most criminal acts as soon as we had a better understanding of the neurological impact on decision making. Ironically, I was the first to put up my hand—almost as if I could see my fate like an infant's bowed legs unfolding before me. How long will that take? Ten years, the speaker said. As usual I was ahead of my time. I was pretty sure most of my decisions fit into that category. I was not making excuses, but was trying to understand something that made no sense at the time. I have since thought about this repeatedly. It was the nexus of my current research. How does someone do something they know is wrong and that they don't want to do? Why can't they see the consequences of their actions before they happen?

But still I didn't know him, I would tell them. He was a stranger—to me, at least. What would be the point in searching for someone you didn't know? They would say. Denial! Not a fucking river in Egypt, but, in fact, the best place in the world. Number one, the magazines raved, lived in by people the world over. Top ten on Reddit.

In the best of all possible worlds, he wouldn't remember me anyway.

He'd be a psychotic. Amnesiac. Concussive. Dead.

Or maybe he didn't give a shit. Did this so often I was just a smudge of dirt he had washed off, one in a long series of smudges.

But what if Cody, or whatever his name was, did care? Please, I would tell him, understand the level of my jeopardy. Look, I would say, if you do tell anyone about this, I will fucking deny it. Who do you think they'll believe, some kid or a middle-aged female Philosophy professor. A no-brainer, I'd tell him. Who'd want to fuck me anyway? Much less a teenager! Nobody would believe it. Well, let's put this in terms you might understand, I'd tell him. The proof is inside me, and nobody will ever have access to that area of my body again. Keep moving. Nothing to see here, folks. See, nobody wants access. Imagine the Antarctic without penguins. No one is interested.

But I had to wonder.

Who would listen if he did say anything?

LeBec. That's who.

Then one night, the phone rang. "You know who this is," said the voice.

I hung up. It rang again two seconds later.

Again, now, I picked up, asking, "What do you want from me?"

Night after night, that same voice called, but she wasn't getting the reaction she wanted and she decided to up the stakes.

"Just tell me where he is. Please. I beg of you."

"What's your problem? I don't even know you."

"That's a fucking joke." She snorted, then her voice picked up a quick new superiority. "Professor Hanks."

At the sound of my name, my heart stopped.

"What do you want from me?" I asked her.

"Did you touch him?"

The world slammed under layers of ice. The phone roared in my ears. Or maybe it was blood pumping through my head, reminding me that I was still, unfortunately, alive. Finally, I said, "What does that mean?"

"I need to know if you touched him. I need to know if you

put your hands on him," were the last words I heard before I hung up.

Right away, she called back.

"You know I know everything about you, right?"

"I don't know what you're talking about," I rasped, and then hung up.

I stared at the phone until it rang again, then finally unplugged it.

That night, I returned to Lurch, the site of the night it had happened. Behind the bar, the imperious waiter from before was fisting a glass with a cloth. The little pedal spun fast inside me. He stared down at me over a pair of tiny wire frames.

"Is Bobby here?"

"Who? No Bobby here."

"Red beard. Worked here five months ago."

"Don't know any Bobby."

"He was the bartender that night you were working the floor." I circled my finger around my chin: the universal beard symbol.

"If you mean Chris, he doesn't work here anymore."

I worried what my neighbours may have heard or seen. When I got back from Lurch, I knocked on the door. Tetrault squeezed his face out between door and frame. "What?" A tie draped over his shoulders. His eyes flicked back inside his apartment. Voices. A crack of bright music. The bubble and incongruity of the peculiar and misanthropic Tetrault. Even with my own life dissolving, the potential of life still amazed me. Tetrault became a symbol of hope I'd secreted deep within myself.

Then from his apartment, a man's voice called out, "Don't move!" trailed by some tinny music, and I realized it was only the TV.

"I'm missing my show," Tetrault said with a hollow whine.

A familiar irritation rubbed me as if I'd just discovered an old sock under the baseboards. I wanted to punish Tetrault. I hardened my voice. Tetrault sawed from foot to foot. "Did you happen to notice anything strange on our floor?"

"When?"

"Anytime."

"Such as?"

"Strange noises or goings on?"

He looked at me closely, then withdrew into his suite. I walked from my apartment to the university then from the university to my apartment. Always looking left and right. Only getting a few hours sleep each night.

I checked the area around the university, outside Lurch again, the forest, the area outside the *Anciana Madre*, but was too scared to enter, driving around night after night, epitomizing the defining quality of the academic. Rigid, narrow mental trajectories, treading the same roads as I contacted pulsing midnight hives of hospitals, motels, police stations, faking a professorial inquiry. "Has a boy turned up? Any boy? Alive or dead? It doesn't matter." The answers always the same, "No, Ma'am," or "We can't release that information," or "Are you a member of the family?"

And with only the name Cody to go by, I couldn't contact the hospitals, try to look him up in the central registry data, make inquiries at the social security office.

I explored every way of tracking him down. Had to examine everything, so that even my brain became a point of inquiry. The incident dropped inside me repeatedly with the weight of fear, disgust, and bewilderment at the unpredictability of my own behaviour.

I came upon a young bearded man with bright blue eyes, loitering near the stairwell. "Seen anything strange around here?" I asked him. He looked at me warily as his expression hardened until I wondered about the others.

They included:

a cafeteria worker who left remainders of flattened and desiccated muffins out in the hall;

Neil, the night manager;

a Philosophy major with a plaid scarf and a long tattered tweed coat who often leaned against the wall near the stairwell, scanning the girls with a mopey, lost, and dogged expression;

a cleaner with pale belligerent eyes whose cart clacked through the halls.

I HADN'T NOTICED these people before, but they now held a threatening power over me. I wasn't going to talk to anyone about him. Then one day Neil clanked past me with his ring of keys, his walkie-talkie clipped to his belt. "Hey!" His voice came at me like someone reaching out through a fog. I stopped. "Have you seen anyone hanging out here?" He thumbed in the direction of the stairwell.

I could hear my voice strain. "A lot of people hang out here."

He nodded. "It's this kid. Skinny. Black hair."

"They're all kids."

"No, young. Definitely not an adult. I'm a little concerned. He was living here." He pointed to the stairwell again.

"I can't do this now." I jabbed at my wrist.

I searched for Cody to and from work, forcing myself to focus on the regime of endless meetings and colloquia, which held for me no significance.

Every one of my cells focused, galvanized for danger.

God, let him not tell, I murmured as I retraced my steps even though, with my perfectly logical, rational mind, I did not believe in God.

Just as the brilliant and esteemed genius, my mentor, didn't tell while he was devising his groundbreaking theory of universal ethics. Cut me by the five points of that star. Each point as sharp as the knife that had sliced life from inside me.

"Christ, Del, nobody died," the stupid genius had said. "And now you're free to get into any university your little heart desires."

Those words still interposed with my fears about LeBec, and the tenure that hung in the balance between me and the boy.

I stood at the window of my apartment watching for Cody while under the streetlights the raindrops pulsed against the window glass.

"Look at you. Just look at you, letting a child ruin your life."

"I guess it had to happen sooner or later."

"Well, at least you would've had something to show for it."

"Like I'd give you the satisfaction."

"Looks like you've got nothing, and now I'm dead."

"Well, at least that's something."

I took precautionary measures not to arouse suspicion, making calls in the lobby of a hotel—rather than from my apartment or cell phone—where the call could not be traced, specifically a Ramada. The lobby still hosted a bank of payphones. A single bored concierge stared into space next to a bowl of apples.

A terminal disease afflicted the world. Geriatric Australian

tourists, oblivious to my crisis, clacked and clucked outside, waiting for their tour bus with pale blank eyes, frizzled greyish-blond
hair, and flowering melanomas.

I walked and traced those strange twisted trajectories as the
beams of headlights cut the rain in every direction. My heart
sank with each step, deeper into this place with its skinny glass
buildings, its newly created little neighbourhoods, each one
with its own fake New York, West Coast surfer, or German
hamlet facade. Each formed some variation on this tiny hideous
trifecta, each neighborhood shuddered in the black rain.

In the 12th century, the theologian Alain de Lille (likely influenced in the third century by the Corpus Hermeticum,
which itself was likely influenced even earlier by Plato, who
himself may have been influenced by Parmenides, who himself
may have been influenced by the rhapsodist Xenophanes of
Colophon) wrote that, "God is an intelligible sphere whose
center is everywhere and whose circumference is nowhere." In
1584, Giordano Bruno wrote, "The center of the universe is
everywhere and its circumference is nowhere." And in the 17th
century, Pascal said the same thing as the others, but instead
of God, he was talking about nature.

I thought of all this as I continued to gaze past the nearby
forest as it glistened blackly, creeping between the lacunae of
the fencing and the metal grating. The rainforest pulsed and
effused with the sweetness of life, death, and rain. One night
driving around the city my cell phone dinged with notifica-
tions. A series of texts surged out of the darkness.

Come

I'm #rubble

Help

Later when I could finally pull over to return the texts, I

wasn't getting a response. I received an error message, this number doesn't receive text messages. I sent a ? And then the word Hello? I received the following message: "Unable to process request. You have probably replied to an expired message."

I called my cellular provider.

"What did it say?" a man asked me.

"It said message expired."

"It was probably a burner."

"Excuse me?"

"Short term. A throw away."

"Who would throw away a phone?"

"A good question worthy of your consideration."

"Really? And why is that? How would the police find someone?"

"Bingo! Ma'am, have I satisfied the reason for your call today?"

I found myself under the moonlight with a flashlight, skirting the forest's mouth, my feet crushing the red carnations, those now long-dead flowers. Their flounces. Throbbing red pistils. Strewn around the areole to honour the dead. Could not bring myself to enter the forest. Didn't want to find something and then have to report back to someone about it. More flowers crumpled further ahead at the claw foot of a light post as I made my way back to my office. A yellow nylon cord tightened around the post snapped me in the face as I passed the outdoor pool. Shouts and practice shots mingled with the smell of chlorine in the wet night air. A rush of bubbles. The glint of a red bathing suit shimmered like a streak of menstrual blood along the robin's-egg-blue basin.

I yearned to contact Tanis, dying now, preoccupied with her flotilla of life support machines. The group email arrived, announcing her transition to the next phase.

I couldn't bother even my one ally now. My only friend.

Tanis Dodge glinted, flashed. Coruscated as a lozenge. Embedded in palliative care, a building known for its proximity to the condemned River Heights mental hospital, a location for TV shoots. Tanis's malignancy metastasized beyond the brain stem. Chemotherapy and radiation husked with her name.

The ulceration or break in the skin resembled a birthmark. Fingers reached down to perform its nasty work, spreading beyond the layers of flesh.

She'd returned to the hospital for the last time. I avoided Tanis. Had few resources to manage her anxiety.

My one ally no longer here to help, no longer here to tell.

I already let slip one word too many about John McGilvery.

I'd never breathe a word about Cody.

And with my acute sense for the hideous, I now suspected Tanis, with her slow shift and withdrawal from the living, having nothing left to lose; as well as our last strange meeting, she may have cultivated feelings of loathing toward me.

But what I long feared was now happening faster than anticipated. LeBec had leveraged herself into a more pointed position with Denke.

I speculated that my file was still before the committee. They were meeting, nobody had told me when, and my colleagues took pleasure in the obsequious smile they forced me to produce every time I had to acknowledge one of them.

They spoke in low covert voices, eyes flicking to the sides.

I witnessed procedural changes as our institution galvanized for more meaningful engagement.

McGilvery had given me that same look. Eyes narrowing. A warning!

Careful!

Too late.

Black sky. Flickering veins of light. Rainwater fizzling the electrical wires. Trudging home each night. Didn't touch towel. Poor sad towel, still clinging to the bathroom rack, even as this moon glinted around me.

One day at the end of March, I came home to track the muddy footprints down the hall to my suite. Handprints crawled up my door. Krevice on all fours. Bucket and sponge. Head churned down to the floor. "Del! What the fuck!" she said as soon as she saw my feet.

"Who did this?"

"Nobody saw who did it. We can't have this. This is a respectable building." She didn't look at me as the muscles under her robe, two enormous hams, moved back and forth.

"I'm sorry, I said. "It won't happen again."

"It better not," she said. "Next time is the last time. I'm calling the police."

"I assure you, you won't need to worry. I apologize for this inconvenience."

"Tell your guests to use the goddamn mat."

No matter how hard I stared at it, the phone didn't ring again, intensifying my fears. The apartment grew frightening, cold, and I didn't want to stay there anymore. But aside from my nightly search, I had no choice but to return back to where it had happened.

I dragged myself back and forth from my apartment to the university. I drank my espresso out of a paper cup, fondling my fate with both fingers. The black shapes rose in the distance. Some were buildings, and some were mountains.

Yet as the sensory details heightened, the world became hazy. Distant. Through the halls of the university came a strong antiseptic smell that I associated with bodily wastes. I stood in line at The Perk.

"Do you smell something?" I asked the woman ahead of me.

She gave me with a watery smile. I had an urge to insult her, but only after she had picked up a goblet of green Jell-O and moved forward with her tray.

To underscore my situation, a crippling fear overcame me, and with this realization the rigidity of my perspective shifted until it broke apart. I walked around in a haze of numb detachment. A wall came down and shut out every other feeling. I carried that sick, vaguely familiar sensation around with me. The smells and tastes, all my sensory affects, heightened and wavered in that strange way that separates the host from the outside world, so the host can focus on the tiny parasite within.

I hadn't even realized that months had passed with no menstrual cycle.

I no longer kept track of such physiological processes.

I'd never had a reason to. My periods had become irregular, stretching out with no snap back like the elastic on an old pair of underwear. Done and doner! I'd thought.

But now I did the math. Mathematics is pure, true, and never wrong.

I soon deduced that it was too late to do anything about it.

I didn't know what I was supposed to do.

All these years invested for nothing.

"Christ, Del, nobody died."

But I didn't know if I could do it. Whenever I tried to work out the problem, my brain buckled under the pressure. I became exhausted. I knew the signs.

What a gift. Unexpected. A miracle! I was horrified. Who was this person whose DNA mingled with my own? This little monster who created an environment of parasitoid within me? The hormones raged. Tearing me away from my rational mind.

That night, I worked against every cell in my body to find a solution. Don't panic. Tenure depends on it. Be practical, just as years earlier, during that faculty lunch when you excused yourself to the lavender confines of a washroom stall to extract a fish bone from your throat. Deal with the ramifications of your mistake. Schedule vacation time. Then return to work. An Associate Professor with tenure. Conduct yourself as usual. Tell them you've gained weight. That you're trying out a new look. Ask them if they like it. If their response isn't positive, they'll feel guilty about it, and they won't ask anymore questions. But they'd never asked anyway. I had no flattering imitators. No one copying my high contrast hair and glasses combo, practical no-nonsense workday attire.

A carton of milk and a steak sat in the refrigerator. The creature pressed inside me. How long had this food been sitting here? I closed the refrigerator by its simulated wood grain handle. Got take out. Drove around, eating out of the paper bag on my lap.

Night after night I fled the precarious corridors of our department into the city to search for this child, the child-father of my tiny parasite.

I knew that masterful genius John McGilvery would say nothing. Not ever.

Destroy evidence!

Even the ultimate evidence.

As the evidence of that stairwell person now grew inside me.

I didn't eat. Sleep. Excluded the outlying neighbourhoods, far away, irrelevant, focusing on the train stations, bus depots, gas stations, and convenience stores whose neon signage glowed out to float in the darkness.

Continued to contact hospitals, morgues, police stations, questioning if I should take ownership of this boy as we now throbbed with the same blood.

You are not making a vision board. Do not stray from task. Let's turn to Murderer. Guess what? It's bad news. He's at the door. Someone's going to die.

IV

PROLAPSED NECK. QUEEN BED. Laptop, glow, the heat, the chitter of emails, message alerts. My fingers take me to tweets and Snapchats, Vines, veins, untapped blue threads. Codes. Pulse. Disappear. Resurface. Remote sites throbbing me to sleep. A shadow passes by the thin crack in the door, calling out from the hall with disgust, "Look at you. Just look at you," before that inevitable release of orgasm. LeBec could trace me to these sites. People hacked through the camera lens. GIFs (Not to be confused with a Gift) me jerking it to online. BM: Beyond MILF. MUDH: Middle Aged Uggo Doing it for Herself. OP: Old Professors. PP: Porn Profs. Next to me on the bed, that tiny lens studied at me until a fist of terror clenched inside.

Then the next day back at work, end of March, one month before the end of our semester, I stood at my office window, watching Denke and LeBec in the parking lot below. They're standing too close together, then they climb into Denke's Saab and drive away.

In seven short months, LeBec has risen in our ranks. Ingratiated herself with faculty, and continually appraised me with expressions of disgust and frustration when I plopped myself down at faculty meetings. The mirror of my banality didn't meet her standards of excellence. Yet I persisted. Trundled along as the world went about its merry march.

And of course, aside from LeBec, what defines stellar? Historically, we can turn back to Annie Money. Torn jeans. Too-tight rock t-shirts. No underwear. Her hair blazed, and beyond the hair, even she blazed with the brightness of the

sun as if a tiny piece of it flickered inside her, or like that bug
that lights up, fireflies or whatever they're called. And how was
it fair anyway that she was both rich and entitled and still got
to look like that? I wanted to be nice. I wanted to like a girl
like that and be nice, but how could I? She made it absolutely
impossible because she a) knew or b) didn't know and was
oblivious. Either way, how could I like her because then she
was either a) a bitch or b) stupid. My only salvation was the
footless or legless or the starving with their swollen hungry
stomachs. I was also okay with the chronic substance user, the
drug addicted and their tweaking and picking of the skin until
that skin blossomed pink, red, blue, or green, or became a sep-
tic blood stream infection requiring a PICC line going straight
to the heart. As long as they were suffering. I wouldn't, for example, have wanted to know the recovered, perfectionistic, and
superior. Nor even the drug addicted if they were enjoying
being a drug addict or a chronic user who hadn't destroyed
their life. Likewise, at the university I could only like the ones
like me: the unstellars. We are as a people nice. We watch our
backs, so as not to get stabbed, garroted or stuck with a shiv.
We are fearful. And the fear can actually erase the niceness.
Make us vicious, vindictive against our nature. We put on an
act for survival. That overused smile that makes us look like
our faces will crack. When we finally get home and look in a
mirror, all we see is our prolapsed necks and our collapsed
faces from over-exertion of the Zygomaticus Major, giving us
that slack-jawed hound dog look. The rest of us could try a
million times and never get close to the stellars. We'll forever
be in the trenches, slugging it out for attention or any scrap
dropped inadvertently from their plates. Now (and this is
something I would never admit to them even if they put a gun

to my head), I was hired on false pretenses. I was a species closer to my mother than the stellars. That is to say, I did not actually fit into stellar, unstellar, or neutral. My mother punched a cash register. The stellars weren't required to teach classes, got plane trips, free dinners at fancy restaurants, and got to stay in hotels and meet famous people. Were interviewed on television. Had opinions people gave a shit about even though they didn't know why. Got a million hits or friends or likes or followers or whatever on social media. Stellars didn't give a shit and were virtually untouchable unless they did something stupid like rape or kill.

Then that ticking time bomb, Cody, bleated up from the darkness.

I came to you

#You promised

Blister jerks on rocket fuss march

Fuck

Help me

I couldn't respond to that. He was insane, I had promised him nothing. Autocorrect, too, was now insane. It had broken loose and was running around the yard.

His circles tightened closer and closer. Soon he would be here. A danger!

I had to find him. I called the number—a different number than the first number. This time a gruff male voice called out through the phone, "Hallo!"

"Is Cody there?"

"Hallo!" Again, followed by a spew of some Eastern European language.

"Cody! Cody!" I called over and over, but got nowhere.

EACH NIGHT, I returned to the edge of the forest. My peregrinations twisted along the path between the university and my apartment. I searched harder, hoped nobody could see me, not my colleagues, not the Committee for Tenure.

Caught now between LeBec and the alleged Cody. I bumbled through each lecture. Fumbled for words with no beginning, a journey I didn't want to make.

When I next stepped out from my office into the hall to do some photocopying I noticed no number on the door of 315, our photocopier room, but a lock.

I couldn't reach Kalli, then made another call to campus security from the beige phone in my office, stomach looping.

"I want to report a lock on door 315."

"Is there a problem?"

"It didn't have a lock until today."

The voice asked for my name and faculty ID. A pause then, "You have not been flagged." A keyboard clicked. "You have not been given access to that room."

"Access? What does that mean?"

"Faculty deemed critical to the project."

"What project?"

"You need to talk to someone who can get you a fob."

I finally reached Kalli. "What's up with 315?"

"Are you in your office?"

Feet scuttled across the linoleum.

We both stared at 315.

"What's wrong with it?"

"It's locked."

"I came all this way for that? I was expecting something interesting."

"What's interesting? Arson?"

"There's a machine in my office if you want to use it."

"When did that happen?" I looked at her carefully. "Faculty usually vote on equipment. Who left me off the email?"

"LeBec and Denke. They have veto."

"Since when?"

"When have I ever known what's going on around here?" Then she lowered her voice, "I think Denke may be grooming LeBec."

"Congratulations, Einstein! Grooming her for what? A barbershop quartet? She doesn't have tenure."

"She has tenure." Kalli blinked.

"When did that happen?" My voice arced sharply. "We have to vote on that."

"There was a meeting—with tenured faculty. They fast tracked her."

It came at me like a punch in the head. I steadied myself. "How nice for us all. What about Denke? Is he stepping down?"

"Yeah, right, like anybody would leave a tenured job."

"Jenks did. And Picot."

"Can I go now?" Kalli said. "I've got mail."

She scuttled back down the hall.

Denke and LeBec had become fused. Conjoined twins so systemically entangled in each other's vital organs that Denke had allowed LeBec to insert herself into his position. Just as the boy and I had transmuted. Cross hatched. Sewn ourselves together. Academia didn't make sense to me anymore. Strange codes. Rules. I no longer understood. Had become a government initiative. A project for the mentally ill, like making license plates. A more expedient financial model than institutionalization. What good did those books do me when I needed them most? Years ago, I had flagged each page and argument I couldn't understand. Mary

Seaman Hall. My dorm. Tiny coronas suspended in the light. The moon. Everything. Splintered into nothing.

And now decades later the adjunct expanded her group. Forced Jenks and Picot into early retirement. Burns denied tenure.

More and more, I stared at the mountains as they faded into the sky. Worried about the tenure, the boy and—pregnancy test after pregnancy test—the month's blood that still never came.

"Christ, Del, nobody died."

I followed the sliver of moon just as I had years ago when I worked for McGilvery and the moon's foil slivered as if cut by a child's hand.

But now it angled, sharp, and knifing.

Danger!

The safety of nature. So misleading. So much a matter of perspective.

I chased that same moon as I toured the night's streets, searching for the boy. I threw myself off parapet after parapet, hoping nobody could see me, especially not the Committee for Tenure. And I didn't even know who they were, that committee. In the meantime, the faculty grew dark and preoccupied. They didn't dare move their eyes. Staggered the halls with confusion, terror, bewilderment.

LeBec inched closer to Denke. By the penultimate meeting, she sat by Denke's side, eyes lowered, as we listened to yet another dismissal.

LeBec lifted her eyes.

I've got your number, Hitler, I conveyed to her telepathically as I held her gaze tight in my own.

A day later Steinmann quit, following a public humiliation via social media by another faculty member, and LeBec lackey, Debbie Green.

We released Steinmann from her duties for jamming the photocopier, generating an environment of "toxic" chaos, and just generally looking clued out.

Shapeless cloud of hair, gold hoop earrings, a blue faux-denim smockish top, beige culottes and ankle boots, orange and blue jute-wrapped bangles. Steinmann picked buns twisted in a thin plastic produce bag with her fingers. Severely depressed. Dogged by shame. Self-loathing. I stared at myself in the warped glass of that funhouse mirror.

My office. Lights out. Considered my fate. Maybe that psychic had made a mistake or maybe I'd misunderstood her. Maybe she meant that the other girl would have both personal and professional success, and I'd have nothing.

Now LeBec sat at the head of the melamine table, Denke at her side like an expensive purse. LeBec delivered the news about Steinmann—even though we all had heard the news a day earlier. Debbie Green turned toward LeBec's glowing face as the rest of us absorbed her words, stunned and terrified.

Abeyance. Youth and death. Muscles and skin sucked by time down into earth. LeBec had created a gateway for her own hires. Summoned young, timorous doctoral students. They followed her orders with the silent obedience of paid assassins.

New people staggered our halls. Exhausted. Overwhelmed. Void of personality. LeBec had them running back and forth doing her little tasks and dirty work.

"Who are they?" I asked.

"Oh, the new hires," Blegg said. "Aren't they amazing?"

I recognized only one. Mary Ann, that tiny fleshy, pink eraser, still doing all the photocopying—but now doing it only for LeBec. Look how LeBec gives purpose to the losers. Who knew where someone like Mary Ann would end up if it weren't for LeBec. Yes, LeBec hid behind her good deeds, so nobody recognized her manipulations. It was strategic genius. She took my very own grad student and appointed her leader of her child army. Look how far the little loser had come. Look at what LeBec could do with her. LeBec *must* be a nice person. She thinks of everyone! The cats, dogs, chickens, losers. But I knew her game, exploiting us all to gain power.

The name Del no longer tinked from her mouth.

The Catastrophic Decision. Not published. Not even close. Notes piled on notes.

Tightened into knots too small to pick apart with even the tiniest fingers. Stay calm. Take medication if necessary. Propranolol, Clonazepam, Ativan.

"Hello, sir," I said to Sudeep, my dealer, whenever I greeted him behind the counter of my pharmacy.

"Here's something you might want to ask your doctor for," he said, giving me a wink. "It brings you down, no S/FX."

"Thanks for the intel," I told him. Keep on walking! No fun for mommy. Not now. Not if I gave any kind of shit about the little dot pumping its life inside me.

But the book, the book, the book. A hero will keep climbing that mountain. Along the way, I witnessed bodies frozen under layers of ice with little flags stuck in the ice. I also witnessed deep slopes, and terrain I could hardly cross. But I will do this—even if it kills me, I thought. And without a Sherpa! I may, like the Donner family, die and need to eat myself to stay alive. Excellent, I thought. That will be good for the book. All those press junkets. You managed to write this book, but in the process you lost a leg and an arm. What happened? Well, it's definitely a delicious story. Folks, if you're eating anything, now is a good time to turn off your TV sets. No, I couldn't even take drugs now because of that little it. I went back to the book anyway, but this time I did it without any assistance from my little friends, the blue, the pink, the white. And even though I hadn't taken them in a long while, if I ever needed them it was now.

The Catastrophic Decision
Cont'd

14a. Moral philosophers say it's wrong to make yourself an exception. But what about in cases of love?

Let's turn to Loser. Let's say you're a totally awkward anti-social loser and you meet another equally malevolent loser. You're both the type of people who have never experienced love, but when the promise of love finally arrives, you can't emotionally navigate its bumpy terrain. What if loving that person means that you would eventually kill them? Is it still better for you and that other person to have known love even though you will both eventually die in a kind of homicide-suicide or is it better to not have known love at all?

What about Sociopathic Child? Let's say you are in your early to mid-forties, and you find out you are pregnant with your one child, but you also have paranormal abilities that can determine that your child will be a sociopath. You have one chance to have a child and, for reasons that are not important, you are unable to adopt, e.g., adoption is too expensive or not open to someone at your age. Should you continue the pregnancy? Is it better to never have loved a child or to have a child who will eventually grow up to be a sociopath and kill you or others? Is it better that the child exists or doesn't exist? Should you kill your own child if you know in advance that the child will grow up to be a totalitarian dictator?

If you look at a photograph of Hitler as a baby, he was adorable. Nobody would believe he'd be responsible for the murder of millions of innocent lives. Or that he was an anti-Semite. (Although, it was hard to know because he couldn't talk yet.)

14b. It's wrong to make yourself an exception.

But what about pure survival?

Now let's return to Bully. I'm ten. There is a bully in the playground. There is also an awkward, weird kid who has become the target of the bully's abuse. I'm just an average mediocre piece of shit kid. Do I bully the awkward, weird kid, so the bully leaves me alone, or do I side with the weird kid and get bullied, too? I'm just trying to survive. How much of a hero do I want to be? All the other kids are terrified of the bully, and support the bully by picking on the weird kid.

Let's say I have paranormal abilities and I find out the bully is Hitler and will one day be responsible for the murder of millions. Should I side with Hitler or should I kill Hitler even if Hitler is a ten-year-old bully on the playground? What if Hitler's hurting and taunting the weird kid means that the kid becomes so scared and dissociated that he or she eventually falls off the climbing structure and dies? Is Hitler then responsible for that kid's death? If I am an obsequious pencil pusher, the supplicating sidekick to the bully, am I also responsible?

Note: Eichmann claimed he always abided by Kant's categorical imperative. During his trials when asked why he agreed to the death of millions, he said he became confused by the words "Final Solution," saying he was tired that day, and had assumed the word final meant everyone had already signed off on it.

I have a hog. I could drop the hog off the climbing structure in the playground and kill Hitler. Even if the other kids get traumatized.

Hitler would kill the hog, but would the hog kill Hitler?

Let's turn to Pirate Ship. On a paper raft we've got a hog and four kids, one being the bully, Hitler. The raft is winding through the black water. It storms and we become lost in the black brackish water. We are hungry. Do we eat the hog? Or is it morally better to eat each other or parts of ourselves? A pirate ship with a flapping black flag nudges up beside us in the black brackish water. Do we give the hog to the pirate ship in exchange for our lives? What would the hog do if it could rationally will it? What if we trade the hog with Hitler? Is it okay to kill and eat Hitler? What would the hog

and/or Hitler do if they could rationally will it? Do
we trade the hog for our safety? Is it acceptable to
use the hog or Hitler as a mere means? We don't
know what will happen to the hog once it is on
board the pirate ship: mascot or food? Does this
necessarily lead to a bad outcome for the hog? And
if we don't know the answer is it, therefore, morally
wrong?

After reading my manuscript, I have decided to further detail
the characteristics of the three categories of academics: stellars, unstellars, neutrals. Stellars: razor-sharp eyes, social
fluidity, facile, funny, whippet-thin, young. Unstellars: flaccid,
old, dowdy, resigned to mediocrity, a drought of publications.
Neutrals: vacillating, pliable, clinging to stellars, but sucked
into the inevitable fate of the unstellars, no governor's pardon
for them, opening their veins to burning, bitter midazolam
death.

They said, "Sorry, Del, I should probably check with the
others first," when I asked if I could join them for lunch. They
skittered back to the group where the eyes of the others grew
dark and tight. They returned, mumbling, "I didn't realize, but
we're actually having a meeting. Maybe another time."

I only had to endure that humiliation once to get the message. After that, I chose to sit by myself. To silently hate them.
I was aware of their little scheme. So interesting how that
lunch rejection had corresponded with LeBec's arrival, the
emails requesting my mandatory participation in LEAP. We
will humiliate. We will drive her out.

How malicious and cruel! Did they think I really wouldn't

see through their little plan to make me leave my own job, or did they not care how much they hurt me? And why me? I watched good TV shows, wore black suits, dyed my hair in high contrast to my funky plastic frames, but it wasn't enough to save me. Let's return to Pirate Ship. One pirate ship. The stellars and unstellars. The black, brackish water. What if we need the unstellars more than stellars. Maybe the research of the unstellars has more longevity than that of the stellars whose work loses potency and value over time. Or maybe unstellars are nice. Turn to Hog. Stellers. Unstellers. Pirate ship. Black, brackish water. Hog helicopered and dropped onto unstellers. Hog used to knock out unstellers, making room for more stellers. How do we justify repeatedly using the hog to save the others? How will we make it to the Kingdom of Ends?

THE FOCUS WAS not my tenure anymore. I just worked on my book the whole time. I worried I couldn't get it done in time. That it wasn't going to happen, no matter what I did. I isolated myself from everyone. I drove around then locked myself in my office and worked on it. I didn't want to go to the faculty meeting. I didn't care anymore. But of course I went. Don't give up. Don't ever give up.

By the first week of April, I was almost five months pregnant. It was now the last week of our winter semester. Good-bye parties clambered up and down the floor of our department as we conducted our final classes. I still hadn't heard about my tenure.

I didn't receive an email, but there was still a chance. Nobody had told me otherwise. Did I not deserve, at minimum, a letter informing me that it was over?

With tenure still looming, it was time for a re-do. I had to assert my presence. The white dress from Fruman's had hung in my closet for months. As I wriggled into it, a surge and a wave moved inside me. I put my hand over it cautiously as another wave followed it.

It wasn't a wedding dress, more like an adult version of an infant christening dress, but it would be the only time Tanis would see me in something marginally close to bridal wear. The dress cushioned against my apprehension. I couldn't witness Tanis in her desiccated state. Steady as an old hen. Please, please let my secrets die with her. The narrowest silver lining.

I cringed past bleak doorways of the palliative care ward, down the long dim hospital hall, hushed nurses, terrified families, silent and vibrating as they awaited the shift to the next stage.

When I emerged from the dark hole of the doorway, LeBec hovered over Tanis's bed. They both flinched back in surprise, then exchanged a quick, conspiratorial look.

"I've got to get back," said LeBec acerbically.

She wore one of her twitchy little outfits. Didn't even have the sense to wear something normal. A stripper, just what every person needs while they're dying. Is this the new Jesus shepherding us through the golden arches? LeBec pinched her lips. Didn't meet my eyes.

"See you later, Helene," I said brightly as she crushed past me out the door.

"What was that?" My gaze darkened in LeBec's shadow. "It's so grade eight."

Tanis lay rigidly in bed. The chemical smell. That other smell. Bodily wastes. The dim lights. She was emaciated. The bones pointed out in her face. Cheek hollows rising, separating strange dark islands. Her staring eyes hardly moved in their sockets. My face. My own hideous malignancy struggled to contain itself.

The boy. My book. The relationship with McGilvery. Everything else.

As her life slipped away, her senses to perceive life became more acute. She tightened her lips. Nudged her eyes at the beige melamine slider. "Water," she husked.

I passed her the plastic cup of melted ice. Bent the straw to her raw, red mouth. She gave a suck. Pulled back. Stared at me with an infant's wonder.

The machines were grinding. She wore pyjamas with cartoon characters stamped into the material. Walls taped with cartoon animals. A vase of flowers. A petal skin had dropped. Curled to its side. A television articulated to the wall by a mechanical arm. Finally, a friend! A crust of my resistance crumbled away.

"How many times has she been by?"

"Who?" she rasped.

"Helene."

"Does it matter?"

"You mean she's been here more than once?"

I could feel my mouth twist. "Of course she has time for hospital visits. She hired an entire fleet of obsequious little ass kissers. You wouldn't recognize the department. She has them doing everything for her."

Tanis struggled through those long, bleak tunnels of eyes.

"I'm sorry I couldn't come sooner," I said.

"What's up, Del?"

"What do you mean?"

The hard angularity of her voice scared me. I couldn't take my eyes off the curved spine of that almost dead petal. A single vein stood out from the white flesh, still trying to feed itself even though it knew it was dying. I wanted to bury my head in the lap of her blankets and cry. But instead I just said, "I need you to help me."

"Del, have you been up all night again?"

"What does that mean?" My voice sharpened. "Helene is stacking and purging. Jenks, Picot, Gagne, Steinmann. One mistake and she uses that to galvanize the faculty against them. Do you even know what's going on? She's taken over half of Eastern Europe. Russia and England are terrified." I was trying to elicit a reaction from her, but she didn't seem to have the energy or the inclination to dredge it up.

Finally, she said, "I get the emails."

"Does LeBec want to replace me with Debbie Green?"

My eyes burned. My voice ached and whined hideously.

"Even if she wanted to do it, she'd never say that."

LeBec had somehow managed to turn Tanis.

"Is this because I never came to visit?"

She sighed. "Del," she began.

"Nice. I suppose she's been in here emptying your colostomy bag. You could have warned me that she replaced the real you with one of them."

Her voice splintered. "It sounds like you're having a hard time."

"It's not just my hard time."

"Del, pull yourself together."

"Really? I've got one word for you. Gaslight. It's not a great movie. But it's exactly what's going on. I didn't think she could get to you, too."

Her body retracted. Machines hissed. Fluids eased through tubes.

Her voice caught an edge of phlegm. "You might want to take a break." She struggled to get the words out, forcing each with a huff. "Think about the students, colleagues. It's so predatorial. So much clawing for resources. It's like Wild Kingdom."

"You don't think I can handle it."

"You're obviously under stress."

Her voice twisted in that same way, gave me the same look she did at Mahon's when I asked her why she didn't ask me to drive her to the party. It was pity.

"Really?" The word stress suddenly turned into the word insane. "How nice of both of you to take the time for this inventory. Is that how you're going to have me put out? Stress? I don't even think I can get a medical with that."

"There are other chances. Other opportunities."

"Oh my God, Tanis! There are no more chances." I yelled at her.

"Look at what you're going through."

I was streaking the snot on my face. Fear burned inside me. It would make me red and blotchy tomorrow. I didn't give a shit.

"You're a bunch of assholes. You know what I did to get this job. I actually thought this all meant something. I thought we were friends."

She eyed me curiously. "Really?"

I bleated with hot fear as I stood there, blinking at her. I didn't move. Watch it! If you say something cruel, you'll regret it. I wanted to do something destructive. Rip the tubes out of the machines. You're not that kind of person. Just like you're not the kind of person who would kill your mother.

"Can't we talk about this rationally?" I said.

She curled tightly. "I don't want to talk about it."

I'd thought she was my friend. I couldn't trust anyone, and now I never would.

"Well, I guess I made a mistake."

Tears bleared Tanis. The room. "So, that's it? Is that how you want to leave this?" I said.

She tilted her eyes at me. They were creamy with pain. "Take care, Del."

I compressed my sorrow. "Whatever. Take care."

She churned her face into her pillow.

Nailed by despair, I pushed away from the table. I'd really believed she was my friend. I felt like a moron. Then a sharp fear caught me. "Did you tell Helene about McGilvery?"

"What about him?"

"Only everything you swore you'd never tell."

"What? That you emotionally blackmailed your grad advisor into writing all your reference letters?"

"I don't know what you mean by blackmail. It's not so strange for a mentor to help their mentee get an academic position."

"I wouldn't use the word position in relation to McGilvery if I were you."

"What are you insinuating?"

"What do you call it when your mentorship was conducted with you staring at the underside of his desk?"

"Did you tell Helene about that?"

She didn't turn her face from the pillow.

"Is that what you told her?" I couldn't contain my fear. My voice became louder, clipped. "Did you tell anyone about this? And what about my tenure? What's going to happen to that?"

A stout nurse bustled in. Examined a length of tubing. "You have to go."

"You promised you wouldn't say anything!" Tanis still didn't look at me. "That was a real bitch move," I said before the nurse shot me a sharp look.

For five minutes I paced outside the hospital. Patients dragged past me with their IV poles and cigarettes. The conversation had seared me open and all my insides were falling out. I didn't know how to put it all back together. I gathered up everything and kept walking, but it felt like too much, and I was going to drop something. Somebody was going to yell at me, *Lady, you dropped something.* Or maybe someone would even step on whatever I'd dropped. Then I realized that when I was little I'd often make a pact with God, whatever God was to me then, that if anyone ever said they loved me I'd be prepared to die if necessary. What I meant was, I'd be prepared to give up years of my life just hear someone say that to me and really mean it. But now I knew that would never happen.

When I phoned Menzer, his receptionist said, "You're no longer a patient." Her voice was hard, flat like a tabletop, each word splintered around the edges.

"I need to talk to Dr. Menzer."

"The doctor is not available," she said.

"It's an emergency."

She sighed, and something inside me curled and tightened.

"Del, if I had a dime for every time you've said that."

"I know," I said.

"You don't know. You've called every day for a month." Her voice sounded cruel. I didn't understand how someone like that had a job with the public.

"Why are you such a bitch? Don't you have anything better to do than hurt people?" The words pitched out of my mouth before I pressed the END CALL on my cell.

I walked away past the hospital toward my car.

"Look at you! Just look at you! Feeling sorry for yourself around the cancerous. Don't bring that infectious attitude around here."

"Cancer isn't infectious, you moron!"

"Well, I guess the chickens have come home to roost."

"The only thing that's come is the rooster, and I'm fucked."

BACK AT THE university, I walked down the long black hall through the tunnel toward the door of the lecture theatre. I'm now officially off-brand, I thought, as I arrived in the dress. Faculty held their gaze on me, but nobody commented on my bold fashion departure.

I had a class to teach, the last one of the term. Five seconds to pull it together.

The yellow lights bobbled high above me like dark bottles of urine.

On the way, I bumped into Blegg who was obviously cutting through the tunnel to Philosophy. It was the first time in weeks a colleague had approached me.

"Hey! Did you hear? They found some strange kid hanging around in the corridors. They escorted him off the campus."

"Where did they take him?"

"Don't know, but apparently he broke away and escaped." She opened a box of powdered donuts and smiled. "Love Joy?"

I pushed past Blegg and trudged back down the long hall all the way through the tunnel to the door of the lecture theatre. Glanced over to the hole under the stairwell on my way.

My hand froze on the door handle. The class had already begun. I pushed the door open and just stood there.

A skinny man I didn't recognize skittered over. Razor burn pimpled his scrawny neck, punctuated by a pointed Adam's apple. His arms dangled like a mobile.

"What's up?"

"What do you mean, what's up? This is my class."

"Excuse me?"

"I'm supposed to be teaching this class."

He cocked his head. "Denke told me you were sick."

"He must be confused. It's obviously a scheduling mistake."

He squeezed the doorframe until the skin of his fingers whitened and he lingered at the door for a minute before he left, watching me as I took my place behind the lectern. The students packed in their tight rows along the graduated floor. I blurred through my words. Something separated me from myself. Like a Kleenex, one ply pulled apart from another. A hum filled the lecture theatre. Nobody moved. I gripped the lectern. My legs buckled. "Continuing from my conclusion of last week's discussion, we have a moral world that the problems speak to. What should we do in moral cases where these problems may apply?"

At the front of the room, a greasy little black-haired nerd with a tiny rat face raised a hand, "I'm wondering if thought experiments create an environment where we are not addressing serious social issues like government regulations and expenditures."

As I focused to take in his comment, I felt strangely irked. The nerd shimmered too brightly. I widened my gaze, and the entire class shimmered behind him.

"We are not addressing that here."

The nerd stood up. "But you specifically asked," the little shit was reading his notes now, "'What should we do in moral cases where these problems may apply?'"

A student with alarmed eyes behind square glasses too big for her face called out, "Are you okay?"

The walls of my brain collapsed as I slid, grasping the edges of the lectern.

Then another shouted out, "Professor Hanks, are you okay?" as I bolted out the door, down the corridor and then through the tunnel across to the philosophy building to my office where a cluster of graduate students drank from tiny plastic glasses, flashing with light and sharp, shrill laughter. I ran between them just as LeBec turned, reached out, clasped my arm with her hand. "Hi Del," she said acerbically.

Something gave way. LeBec stood in front of me. Vomit sprayed across her shirt. Her face. Strings of vomit dangling from her hair.

I slid, then crumpled to the floor. People clustered around. Legs caged me.

"Are you all right?" someone asked.

I looked up. They were crowding around as LeBec wiped her face with the back of her arm.

"Are you all right?" Denke asked LeBec. Then perfunctorily reached down and jerked me up by both arms. "Let's go," his voice whipped. "Come, now."

Weakly, I waved him away.

Nobody spoke. Nobody moved.

"She's sick," Blegg said. "She didn't even want a donut." Then she turned to me. "Do you want us to call someone for you?"

I shook my head. Their eyes were hard. Punitive.

I chose my words carefully the way one would pick up shards of glass from the floor. "I've been ill," I told them. I forgot I was wearing the dress. It flounced, foaming out around me on the floor.

Not a single pair of eyes softened toward me.

I touched my face. Pulled my hand back to see the blood on my fingers.

Denke's hand clasped my shoulder. I wrenched from his grip. Tried to drag myself away as a trail of low, serious voices murmured and caught behind me.

"Be careful!" LeBec called out sharply. LeBec grabbed me, her hands touching my shirt, skin. Then Blegg grabbed me up by the other side. I tried to push them away.

"Don't push her," a voice lashed. "She's pregnant." Two unidentified faculty glared at me and pointed at Blegg's stomach.

"I'm fine," Blegg called out.

Blegg and LeBec dragged me down the hall, their hands pressing into my arms. I wrenched away from them. I hissed, "Do not touch me." I ached to yell out at both of them. But I would not lose my decorum.

"Drunk!" someone said.

I broke away. Steadied myself. Took a step. Slipped. Slipped again. A voice shouted out, "Oh, my God!" Another yelled out, "Holy Fuck!" as I scrambled up again to run, slip-sliding my way across the floor, their voices faded behind me.

Against the toilet stall, I bunched up like fence wire, my legs buckling, the entire bottom half of my body contracting, a vice so tight I couldn't get out. My hands flattened against both sides of the cubicle walls. Feet scuttled past and disappeared, followed by a group of students who jammed into the bathroom. Wavering through my tears, through the slit between the door and frame, several girls crowded around the mirror.

From outside, Kalli called, "I saw her go this way. Del?"

Then another voice, authoritative, female struck out at me. One I didn't recognize, "Del, open this door. We want to talk to you."

I held in each throb of my heart as the feet pattered further and further away.

I slipped out. Crossed the quad over to the parkade. The rain slashed. Keys clinked, flashed in my hand.

———

I got in my Jetta and drove away. Willed the traffic lights to turn faster. The wipers beat against the glass. Trees, streets, cars smeared into each other. The world about to tear apart, about to tear me apart street by street. I drove until it was almost dark and I was almost out of gas. As I cut a tight corner to return to my apartment, I somehow lost control of the car, grazed a telephone pole, fence, brick wall, and sliced off the front fender. Pulled my face up from the dashboard, held onto the door. My dress snagged on the corner of the door as I staggered out, crawling onto the earth on all bleeding fours, a length of the dress had stripped off, dragging behind me. The Jetta was mangled and destroyed. I could probably get twenty bucks. Fuck it, I thought, as I lurched my way through street after street. The cold numbed my hands. My face angled in the black mirrors of windows, the glass doors, and even the puddles below.

Heading toward me a man pushed a stroller with a plaster baby head mounted like a talisman. One hollowed out broken eye. The other an opaque cataractal blue marble. Dirty china rose painted cheeks. Tiny perforated rows of skull.

I shivered, shook, clenched the dress covered in dirt, blood. Those strips of skin, slapping my body. Street by street. Strange neighbourhoods wound out and opened into the lights of stranger neighbourhoods. I stumbled, then crawled a little into the rain. It darkened and weighed down my dress, pasted hair against my eyes. Drove me to the road into the lights, scissoring between the rushing cars.

The wind blew the silver needles of rain across the headlights. I walked along the narrow lip of the road. Passed a series of industrial buildings.

Vehicles came. Went. Horns sheared layers off the night

air as they swerved to pass me. Big trucks seared past as I walked along the gravel. I sat on the edge, shivering in the cold.

"Look at you. Just look at you."

"Things aren't working out at the university."

"You should've gone to secretary school."

"Well, I didn't."

"You'll need to come to terms with that decision."

"I have. I've done that already."

She sucked in her breath. "You can always teach high school, like Clint."

"Clint doesn't have a PhD. Clint didn't work his ass off for a PhD like I did."

She clucked. "Well, I hope it was worth it."

"Don't start with me."

"You put in a respectable effort," she said. "Why should you be an exception to the rule?"

"Why shouldn't I be an exception, Mother?"

Street after street as the city grew and swallowed me, and with each neighbourhood, the same names rippled out in front of me: Starbucks. Body Shop. Subway. McDonalds. Mr. Lube. 7-Eleven. Supercuts. JugOJuice.

My legs ached as I limped through the streets, not knowing where I was.

Reflected on both sides, I limped past glass-lined streets into the rough area near the university. Somehow, against all my efforts, I'd made a full circle from where I'd abandoned the car. I passed the curve of the water where the waves lapped. Rain fell like a tawdry silver-beaded curtain over the apartments named Ocean Spray and Florida as the sweet rotting trees pushed out their products of conception.

Then I slipped and clutched the edge of a building, leaning

against it, the ground wet and hard under my knees. I staggered up and crawled along the pavement, white dress half-torn, gauze, bow scratched off, legs trembling so hard I thought they would break. Pulled myself into the 7-Eleven parking lot. Sprawled on the ground, shivering. A patrol car circled the block twice then slowed.

Two people crossed the lot, who I somehow recognized through the curtain of rain as my students.

They turned. "Are you okay?" They kept asking me.

"You're bleeding." One touched her face. They looked at each other then walked away just as the rapid pulse of a police light tightened around me. A voice yelled out, "Keep moving." Black shapes in the distance rose. The buildings. The mountains.

Just then texts surfaced.

Almost dead now

Phone is crying

Come get me antic mounties

An ciabatta

Madreporitite

Mad respect

An canine

Fuck

Aryan mandala

Fuck

Arsenic madate

The moon ran behind me in the night as I cut through the hard rain and the tall grasses of a vacant lot. Then ran, stumbling all the way down the slope to the sea. I ran along the hard grey water as the waves slapped and the rain fell over the buildings.

My reflection flashed back at me from black windows, more and more light dying away as I ran through those hard, sharp drops.

The moon grew. The world made stark against the darkening sky. Black building after black building. The swelling moonlight spangled the black needles and branches as more of them pricked my cheeks and the last of the buildings dwindled away.

I advanced to penetrate this black hole of a world. With every step, my surroundings shifted. I found myself at the edge of the forest I had passed earlier.

Here, a sign hung from a steel link fence. WARNING: Enter At Your Own Risk.

With this, I knew I was close to the *Anciana Madre*.

Wedging my toes between the wire holes of the fence, I climbed to the top, then stared down, too terrified to raise my leg over the barbs to the other side.

I slipped, and crashed down into the underbrush.

Nutlets birthed from mature nuts. Needles. Bark. Naked, hanging hairy clumps. Fingers sewn tight. Serrated, sharp hands of ferns, cutting and plunging me into the darkest green. The flickering veins in the sky thrust against the driving rain as pieces of moonlight chinked between darkness.

Trees cracked in half. Gnarled stumps. Headless. Limbs thrown wide. Exposed.

I strained against the rain as the swish and sigh of the natural world sucked me deeper.

Now I almost believed in signs. Even though I knew he must be crouched in some doorway of the streets, I pushed my way through a tangle of branches to prints in the mud. The same that had crawled up my door. Followed the trail, parting and plunging to an opening. Something soft white throbbed. Then glowed. I knelt. Touched a bone. Rib bones. Fibula. Skull. Broken. White. Old bones, clean, and bleached by the sun.

I pushed on. My cone photoreceptors turned green into black, black into levels of grey and lacunae. I muscled up the foot of a ridge. The ground became uneven.

My knees buckled until my foot twisted at the ankle. I tried to stand up again.

The pain shot up my leg. The tracks stopped.

As I ran as fast as my twisted foot would allow, my eyes caught on the *Anciana Madre*, that cluster of pines shivering in the distance, and something, maybe a person lying face down, maybe sleeping, far in the dark, gripping the ground in the black rain, so hard to tell.

V.

WHEN IT WAS all over, my esteemed mentor had taken my wrists with a judicious pressure. "I didn't want anything to come between us. I was afraid. Do you understand?"

"Afraid?" I said.

"Don't confuse an individual's internal life with his external presentation. The disparity will surprise and disappoint you."

"I understand."

But it didn't really happen like that.

Because I had a reception at Grad Phil to attend. Had pre-occupied myself with jumping from parapets. Counting them one, two, three. On and off parapets of all kinds and dimensions. Concrete parkades, and platforms, and ramps.

Every night in the streets I ran. My skin built up layers of slick, greasy sweat, thinking others must have tried this before.

"You must work in partnership with God. Reach out your hand," said Pastor Kevin at the Church of the Neighbourhood Friends.

"Reach out your hand to hold God's hand and enter the Kingdom of Ends."

People saw the short chubby girl with the blond practical cut and the thick glasses running down the street. They speculated that she was probably trying to lose weight. Blotchy. Shiny. Glasses sliding down her snub, pushed-up pug nose as she nudged them up to the bridge, holding them in place with her hand as she ran.

Who knew that in years to come, this girl would be the same girl from Wilbur Smith who received a full-ride to that acclaimed Ivy League university, turned into an Assistant Professor of Philosophy, tenure track. Because back then, they'd thought, there she goes, running in pursuit of some boy. So sad, pathetic, futile since boys of that age, and later even men, don't have the visual imaginations to retrain the mind and perceive potential in one such as her.

AFTER DAYS OF wandering the streets, apprehensive, frightened, wanting to sob, to plead, "Please, come get me. Please." I had stopped eating, sleeping.

"Look at you. Just look at you."

Having made every effort to avoid such a situation. Having made the appointment. Having gone to the Women's Health Centre. Having suffered the humiliation. Then having walked past those signs. The ones for birth control. The ones for disease. Having lain on the hard table. Then having opened my legs. Having permitted the woman in the white gown to put something cold inside.

"Oh, my God!" the woman gasped. "Are you a virgin?"

But no! Not a virgin. Not anymore.

And the Women's Health Centre, during a particularly reactionary phase, a right wing administration and a backlash against abortion and birth control from religious and pro-life pressure groups, had made the executive decision not to put the young woman (looking more like a girl, like a squat, fat girl, an ugly doll, a troll, the flat, plain face, eyes pinched together, inexpressive, blank) on the pill because she was too inexperienced, immature, for intercourse, so how could she negotiate the regime of oral contraception. Thus, it was recorded in her chart, deemed a poor candidate.

"What will I do?" The girl honked into her hands while

the kindly middle-aged nurse said, "Honey, just ask him to use a safe."

But something bad had happened. Like those teenagers on Donahue who didn't realize they were pregnant until they had to go to the bathroom and had a baby.

I reached to touch what grew inside. As dark and cold as metal. My hand drew back. Because I just wanted to go to school like a normal girl and do normal girl things like eat candy and watch TV. I didn't like the word baby. Too round. Too dumb. The scale within me too broken, so that school, Immanuel Kant, even a package of sickly sweet Tom Thumbs and chocolaty Chuckanuts, even church, even Pastor Kevin and *Gilligan's Island* equaled a baby in weight and value. I wanted to go back to before I got pregnant even if it meant I had to re-listen to all those conversations between Annie Money and those stupid girls from behind my book.

I wouldn't attend class that day.

I would have a procedure as remote and facile as a model having a stubborn corn sliced off her toe with the edge of the surgeon's sparkling silver blade.

I couldn't decide what to do.

After two months, three months, three and one half, then four, the geometric arcs I'd carved, tightened between here and there. I returned to the clinic again and again.

"Soon it will be too late to do anything. You get my drift?"

She had an English accent and giant square horse teeth and had given me her name in a moment of feigned intimacy. My brain registered the name as "Morning."

I didn't feel like asking the woman in the oversized t-shirt with the worried red clown curls and the tiny scalp patches to repeat herself the way she repeated, "You get my drift? You don't want to wake up one day with a baby, Susan. You get my drift?"

I gave the clinic his ex-wife's name instead of my own.

"I didn't think it would happen," I kept saying.

"Did you have intercourse?"

"Yes."

"If you have intercourse then you could get pregnant?"

"Really?"

"Cause and effect, Susan."

"I just wanted him to love me."

"Do you want a baby, Susan?"

"I don't know what that means." Then I looked at her. "I feel weird and sick. I've never felt like this before. Does this mean I don't want it?"

But the fat girl didn't really think about the baby part. Then once it happened, she like seriously freaked out. Funny, years later I found out about a mental disorder called depersonalization, a kind of dissociative disorder instigated sometimes by the change in hormones. At the bottom of the well, I couldn't access the feelings. If I had been in a lover's quarrel during that strange time, would I have committed a murder that would've landed me in jail? Later I often wondered, but what I did do was legal and I couldn't be punished. You were supposed to love your baby or not love it—in which case, *blammo!* The magazines didn't know about depersonalization then, but neither did old clown curls.

"Nobody died," he said.

Like he loved me.

A scholarship winner from Wilbur Smith.

He had a wife, Susan. She was gone, but still. And the book.

Wandering down the street in a haze. So extraordinarily wet

that spring. Just like now—here—a child's lifetime later in the rainforest. The rain had made the light—the neon and the other lights—vibrate and tremble against the black sky.

Back then I'd thrown myself off parapet after parapet. Stairwells, parkades, even dumpsters, thinking I must go to the reception for Grad Phil.

"Grad school awaits you," he'd said.

Maybe a chance, a very slight chance, they'd accept you into this program, this very prestigious program, arrangements made, machinations put in place by my very esteemed mentor, John McGilvery.

Don't stand too close. Susan, the bleak blur of a wife.

He had looked at me with that look he'd given me the first time. We'd have this promise. A secret. As tensile as the double chains of a helix, of the DNA, as pure and true and attenuated as a young girl's hymen.

I understood the life of the university. But I could not understand that other life, the one involving a child. No matter how hard I angled, strained, and tried I could not compose a picture in my mind about a life I knew nothing about.

Or as Berkeley says, to exist is to be perceived by the senses.

Hence, it must not exist.

But we will do what's right.

I imagined and hoped that he would say, "Have it."

"Because of the Kingdom of Ends?"

"No," he'd say with conviction, "because it's ours."

Like when I showed up at his office after class. He laughed. Joked with a few people. Kicked them out, pulled the door shut behind me.

But first he saw me, waited, said, "What are you doing here?"

"Dunno."

"Well, come in, damn it. Don't just—"

His voice sharp. Angry as a slap. All my rationality sliding down my face.

"What do you want?" he said. Then seeing my face.

"Are you all right? Christ!" he said. He touched my shoulder with his hand.

After I'd told him, his eyes pinched me in disbelief. He sat in silence. Imploringly, he said, "You can't do this. This is not the time."

"When is the time?" the fat girl asked like a stupid fucking moron.

"My book," he cried. "*The Five Pointed Star.*"

He shoved those words down inside me. They kept bobbing to the surface.

"How did this even happen?" His mouth twitched as if he might cry.

Later that night I felt around for some glint of joy moving around inside me. The metallic cold. It made me retract my hand.

Still. It would be all right.

He had chosen me.

THE MOVIE STAR said, "We had the baby even though we had only known each other for a year. When you know, you just— you know—know."

"If it's love, why wait?"

"I just wanted that little him/me running around."

"You can't question our love."

I crossed the city to the stack at Slaughter where every night in high school my elbows had rounded the cash register, flipping through the pages of *Us, People, Star.* Now I reached back for those magazines I'd stuffed under the cash register, so far back you had to flatten your hand. Slide it deep inside the slot. Those movie star faces now trapped in their squares. Frozen, cracked, and terrified as if off camera someone held a gun to their heads. The pages smelled like Sweet Tarts, mouldering into a bacterial overgrowth.

No, it was just the smell of cheap, glossy magazine ink on its knees as it burrowed its way, clawed its way deeply, and more deeply inside me.

Hormones swirled and tightened. The black foil stretched out further and further until the icy repulsion made me withdraw my hand from that narrow slot.

I couldn't feel anything except the sickles. They cut, pointed, sharp, and moving in a place so cold and dark even a star couldn't exist. As each day passed with no blood on the squares of toilet paper, the limbs flashed whitely. Clung. Clenched. Unwilling to let go no matter how much I willed it.

"YOU CAN'T KEEP coming back. You've got to make a decision."

"You're freaking me out."

They were going to make me have it. "I don't know what to do." I asked, "How many times can you change the appointment?"

"I like you, Susan." Morning held my eyes. "But I think you know the answer."

A grating clamped down so tight I could not fight my way out.

"Do you want to see the heart?"

I jerked my head to the side.

"Would you like to keep the products of conception? Make a ceremony?"

I thrust her away with my eyes.

I jumped on and off the parapets. Nothing felt the same. This dense light caught a ball of dust, shrinking and distant. Viewed from this telescopic lens, this cold sensation thrust me farther from myself.

I had walked back and forth along the parapets. Hoping something beyond me would push me off and kill us both. My hormones elevated, making the layer of skin even more cold, more metallic in a place where rage, sorrow and fear circled. The tiny biting animals ate each other, reproduced, then kept biting and eating.

McGilvery's eyes popped wide open. I stood there, smiling, waiting. His eyes moved, then inverted, far into a distance within himself.

"I thought maybe you'd, you know, want it."

"What are you talking about?"

I looked at him. Leveled by shame. Red hot, with shame. I sat there. Said nothing, smiling so hard my cheeks hurt, just smiling a smile so forced the muscles ached and the tears welled in my eyes.

"Christ, Del, nobody died."

I picked up my things, passed a smudge of students who sat on the floor, slouched against the walls outside his office with their knapsacks.

The next day he left a note on his door. It said he no longer needed my services.

After that, everything else was about managing the pain.

"Christ, Del, nobody died." He laughed that pointed, sharp, derisive, brutal laugh. Because I knew he didn't want to pursue the subject. Because I knew if he had any questions he would either call or write. Of course he never did.

I thought about it every day, rising sweat-soaked in the middle of the night, burning with a rage big enough to do something. I pulled over the blanket, curled for days, trying to figure out what had happened to me and what was going to happen to the baby. "Why won't anyone save us?" I asked it deep down under the blanket. "Why won't anyone tell us what to do?"

"But they are telling us," the baby said.

"Really? I've yet to see evidence of that fact," I told the baby. "I want you, but I don't feel anything," I said. "Make me feel something and I'll keep you. Give me a sign. Anything."

"But you don't believe in signs," the baby said. "Anything I tell you will be a fool's errand." Then it said, "Why don't you go to Pastor Kevin? He loves to discuss such issues as babies and pro-life fucking bullshit."

"Are you fucking nuts?" I told the baby. "What does that nimrod have to say about anything?" But the baby didn't answer. If PK has the answer, then God must exist, so I'll wait for God. This is your chance, God, I said. Sink or swim, buddy. And I rubbed the spot where I thought the little baby circled like a goldfish in a bowl. I rubbed it just in case, as I waited and waited for a sign, my brain twisting and breaking apart under the pressure, waiting for God, Kant, anyone to intervene. But nothing came.

Then every night, running behind the moon, taunting and mean in the sky. My brain froze. The world caught inside me like the headlights of a hostage-taking:

"Yes, everything's fine, Mother. Please, just send the money."

"Look at you. Just look at you. Too stupid to use a safe."

"This isn't World War One. They're called condoms now."

"You won't be living in one of them at this rate."

She'd gloried in my possible and final return to the tiny neighbourhood of resigned workers and exhausted mothers with their red and screaming bundles.

I wouldn't do it. I wouldn't give her the satisfaction.

"You'll end up back home."

I thought about this as I wandered street after street each day, each time steering clear of the clinic, these circles, the axis of this circumference tightening into a little black hole, the prick of a pin too hard to see 'til it had almost grown too late to turn back. It grew inside me. Too cold. Too far away. I couldn't touch it.

The Catastrophic Decision
Conclusion

Let's turn to the Doctrine of Double Effect (Aquinas): It is sometimes permissible to allow something that you foresee might bring about a catastrophe as long as that catastrophe is not intended. I don't want to treat someone as a mere means.

15. How do we parse these complex moral dilemmas?

Let's return to Dress. Do we buy the dress or give the money to charity? I get more joy from the dress than I get from charity. Would we not agree that we should not live in a joyless world?

Now turning to Bully. A wooden box sits on the street. If Hitler is chasing me and my three friends, do I throw the box in front of Hitler, so he doesn't kill me and three people? What if there is a baby in the box and the baby gets hurt? Am I to blame if I don't know there is a baby in the box before I throw it?

Let's turn to Pyramid Scheme. Do I participate to keep the scheme going, so fewer people don't lose their retirement savings?

Let's turn to Chain Letter. If I don't send the chain letter to three other people then the spell won't be broken. Everyone will die of a broken heart. Or have broken kneecaps. Or get cancer. Physical violence will befall you if you don't complete the chain letter. At the very least, people are walking around with massive amounts of anxiety that could cause someone to die. Would that death be my responsibility?

Let's turn to Cult. I am a member of a cult. I thought it was a normal therapy group. Then suddenly I'm not allowed out of the house. I'm asked to cut off contact with family, sell flowers in front of grocery stores and so forth. Do I kill cult leader to escape? What if my attempts to kill cult leader fail and lead to death of other cult members? What if to survive the cult I just pretend to drink the Kool Aid while the other cult members really drink it? To admit to not drinking Kool Aid could result in my death. And yet, while I pretend to drink the Kool Aid, the other cult members are looking at my nodding, smiling, gleeful face while they actually drink their Kool Aid. What is the difference between this kind of moral deception and being forced to murder someone with my own hands?

What if every choice I make is morally wrong, but if I didn't make this choice I would be murdered?

Let's take Oryx. What if we walk down a dusty road and find an oryx. Should we lock the oryx in a cage or do we let it out of the cage knowing that the oryx may get eaten by a lion? What if the lion adopts the oryx? Or what if the lion becomes friends with a cat or what if a cat and a chick become friends or a cat and a guerilla or a horse and a squirrel?

How do we parse these moral questions?

Let's turn to Rat. What if I am part of a drug cartel, and the FBI catches me? They give me a choice: life in prison or ratting out the cartel. If I rat, then a bunch of people could die. Do I save myself or do I sacrifice myself for the greater good? Do I give someone up or do I risk having more people discovered and possibly killed? If I go to prison, I could get revenge-murdered. How important is it for me to save my own life versus the lives of the others?

Let's turn to Drone. There is a war. The kids are poor. A drone flies over the schoolyard. The kids think the drone is a toy, but really it's a consequence of war and it's going to kill innocent children. Do we use the hog to destroy the drone? Do we drop the hog on the drone from a tall building or a climbing structure? We are children and weigh less than the hog. If the hog falls onto the drone, there is a chance the hog will run away after it destroys the drone, thereby saving the three children without hurting the hog?

What should we do in these moral cases? Is there a side constraint that makes the use of any one to save a larger number morally right?

16. Deontological and Utilitarian positions often cloud in the pursuit of answers to these moral questions.

Now let's turn to Horse. At no point when we observe a horse in a gallop, can we see all four points of the horse's legs in the air.

Take for example, Eadweard Muybridge's photographs of Leland Stanford's Kentucky-bred mare Sallie Gardner in motion. Stanford wanted to prove that at some point in a gallop, a horse raises all four feet in the air. Muybridge worked to create a machine.

17. Initially, Muybridge's ambition exceeded his abilities as well as the limits of science and technology. He needed to catch the horse's gallop, but such a gallop could not be caught with the eye and the mind. After much pressure by Stanford, Muybridge's mental resources were finally able to reach his destiny.

Muybridge arranged 24 cameras along a track parallel to the horse's path. Muybridge used these 24 cameras, each 27 inches apart, shutters controlled by trip wires triggered by the horse's legs.

The photographs were taken in succession one twenty-fifth of a second apart, with the shutter speeds calculated to be less than 1/2000 s.

Muybridge invented an instrument that could capture what the human eye could not see in a series of pictures now known as stop motion photography.

Muybridge would eventually murder his much younger wife's lover for ostensibly impregnating her with what would be Muybridge's only son. Muybridge would be acquitted for justifiable homicide as he had head injuries sustained from an earlier stagecoach accident.

Muybridge (born Edward James Muggeridge) changed both his first and last names several times to capture an antiquated resonance. Documents show he went from Muggridge to Muygridge before settling on Muybridge.

Eventually, his name would be misspelled on his tombstone as Eadweard Maybridge. Muybridge's son would eventually become a Texan ranch hand and look exactly like Muybridge.

18A. Still we can pose the question: Where is the clarifying approach between the poles of deontology and utilitarianism?

18B. Here we can turn to the pre-Socratics for answers. Heraclitus says fire is always in the process of becoming something else. We can apply the same principle to stop motion photography.

19. By using technology to change perception, Muybridge shattered the art world. He captured what had been neurologically impossible, freezing time in space, so that reality could now be seized and dissected.

Although Muybridge did manage to catch the point where all four feet of a horse are suspended in the air at the same time, I still can't make sense of this problem of ethical decision-making. Just as with Muybridge, is it possible that we don't yet have the equipment to piece apart and understand how to solve these moral problems? I think and brood obsessively, like a starving animal. In the natural world neurological instruments do not yet exist to catch such nuanced subtleties of thought and experience, making some tragedies truly unavoidable unless we first suffer the consequences.

Even now as I write this my screen pixelates. Each single dot is meaningless, yet together they vibrate at a frequency that creates its own meaning. It's own life.

I, too, am made up of tiny dots that comprise my whole. You cannot use the one as a means. Even if it's the hog. Kill one or kill three.

I don't know where I end and begin or where I end and you begin. We have neither the information nor the tools to stop the horse's legs in motion to discern whether they are, in fact, all four in the air.

Some situations may be too unusual to figure out in advance even with all available instruments of deduction, so that legislation does not yet exist to support our projected understanding of human neurology. The only thing I have is the vision that it takes to create the instruments of deduction, followed by the legislation that will help guide us in our interpretation of human neurological behaviour and its impact on criminality. But what if I don't have the vision? Any projection of the future slips between my fingers no matter how hard I press them together.

20. There is no such thing as black and white. Here and there. Death and life. Moral and amoral. Good and bad. Cat and dog. Grass and fire. You and me. Sanity and insanity. Life and death. Who chooses when one lives and one dies? Who makes such distinctions? At what point do we say, you have gone from the living to the dead? Let's call such bivalent distinctions false. They exist as constructs manufactured by a terrified psyche. How do I differentiate between the real and the unreal? Between good and bad? We can't make something stand still when that idea is a false construct created by a disordered mind. When one commits a crime, who is to decide whether the crime committed is an act of amorality or madness? Can we make a distinction between the amoral and the insane? Increasingly, is it possible that every criminal intent at its base is an act of some kind of insanity that has not yet been defined by an act of legislation, e.g., why would someone in their right mind wear the dress from Fruman's?

Now I wonder, is it possible that, even with all the evidence, some tragedies are unavoidable unless we ourselves have first suffered the consequences?

I have asked myself that same question every day for twenty years. Even with this, I still can't make sense of this problem.

I have grown afraid that I will never come to any understanding before I die. And even then who is to say the understanding cannot come after my death? I continue in the privacy of my office to brood. It has become an obsession, and like a starving animal, I can only think about one thing. One day my book will be complete, and maybe they will understand the brutal sacrifice at the heart of my contribution. I have arrived at nothing. I have tried to turn away and to make sense of my choices and the shape they have given my life and to wonder and speculate as to whether any of this will matter to anyone but me, and yet I can't stop thinking about it.

And who knows how in the future we will neurologically understand the process of decision-making with the advances of science and electromagnetic imaging. I thought about this twenty years ago as, both stunned and bewildered by the possibilities that faced me from both sides, I found myself back at the clinic.

"When it's over, your life will be exactly the same as it was before all this. Do you think you can do that?"

"I don't know. I've never done it before. What does it look like?"

"An alien."

"Really?"

On a cover of the *Weekly World News*, the white spherical creature, fingers dangling like the hands of the junkies I'd seen on Slaughter, was discussing policy with President Reagan on the White House lawn.

"Do you want a baby in nine months, Susan?"

"I already have a baby."

"We don't call it that until it's born."

I didn't believe in God, but there I was on the bridge crying into the black water. Wondering if it would hurt. The black water. The moon rippling across it like a sheet of tin foil. Of course it would hurt, but how much?

"Just count back from ten," the nurse said.

Twilight drugs.

My favourite time of day. Not day or night. Anything could still happen while the dying sun bled the blue out of the sky.

"It's okay, it's okay." The nurse squeezed my hand.

In the dark, my legs spread apart, I slipped down.

Not an alien like they promised. The pouting rosebud. The staring eyes. All four limbs and a head flashing in the dark. The spaces separated. Moved farther apart.

I opened the dark of my legs under the knife of the light. The blood glinted in the moonlight as sharp as stars down my thighs.

I'd finally made it to the *Anciana Madre*, closer than I'd remembered it from the one tour I'd taken six years ago. I moved toward that thing I thought I saw crumpled up in the distance. I walked as fast as I could on one good leg, dragging the other behind.

My eyes flashed to that opening big enough for a man's fist. I snapped the fronds. Pushed myself through the hole. My thighs sticky. Hurt foot bunched in half. The pain in my ankle seared up my leg. All this time, and still I hadn't found him.

Until I finally reached for that crumpled thing, stretching out and clinging to the ground, and clutched in my arms that dog of a sleeping bag.

Then cramps came 'til something warm broke a little, then trickled down my thighs. I couldn't see until I pressed the light on my phone, and then saw a clot there in the blood.

I wanted to take that bit of blood and carry it away.

My hand dipped into the blood, flinching again. Then I picked up the little clot. It beaded. Clung. Then broke to pieces under my finger.

I touched my stomach. Nothing. Not a wave or a flutter. A blister of confusion and sorrow opened. I wanted to lie down forever, but clenched, ached up against the rain and the cold.

I could stand as long as I put most of the weight on the tree. Stripped off a piece of cloth, knotting it to the wound. A little blood oozed through the layers of fabric.

The blood from inside my thighs slicked down. Stuck the skin of my thighs together. The ground crumbled. I fell through a hole.

Turning my face into the earth, I fell asleep, imagining the bugs that would crawl back and forth over my hands and cheeks as the black world filled my mouth and nostrils.

AFTER IT WAS over, I moved out of my dorm away from those girls, crossing town to stay in my old room on Slaughter, lying under the chenille bedspread, the nubs worn. Transparent. I stared at that dark triangle. They never knew why I'd come back. I never told anyone.

I wouldn't leave my room. The rain froze. White lace webbed over all of Slaughter. The crows froze on their wires. The sky thickened with frost.

Behind Clint's door, the stereo thumped and pulsed *Lizzy.* The phone rang. My mother's voice arced, then hung up.

The television changed, grinding out the theme song of a game show. My father opened the refrigerator and yelled, "Where's the Diet Coke?"

"Fridge," my mother yelled back.

"Where?"

"Fridge, goddamn it."

My mother yelled, "Dinner!" My father clomped down the stairs. Clint took his plate to his room, elbowing the door closed.

My mother called up the stairs, "I'm leaving your food in the Tupperware."

One day, the crystalline clumps, those lines of perfect opalescent statues, cracked and melted all over the grass like broken umbrellas. I finally came down.

My mother watched me eat. "Look at you. Just look at you. Nobody's going to marry you. Nobody's going to give you a child." Her eyes darkened, crushed with disappointment. Then I saw, competing under the surface, a tiny knife of pleasure.

I pushed it down where it froze.

Then ten days later, at the reception for Grad Phil, I emerged from the bathroom, hoping to get a glimpse of John McGilvery. Don't talk to him or even stand close to him at faculty events. Not in public. He could never acknowledge us. Especially now.

As I slipped by, he stood there, one hand cupping the bulb of wine, the red liquid edging over the hilt of the glass, as the other crawled up the side of the wall like the branch of a tree spread over the head of that stupid idiot, that Annie Money, for all to see. It almost touched her perfect hair, her perfect body. She had strategically chosen a Laura Ashley dress, *peau de soie* lined in muslin and screen-printed cotton. Her bare little feet tinkled with a gold anklet. Her hair and the anklet caught the light and flashed.

The hormonal haze of pregnancy had cleared gradually like night, and my reasons for what I'd done suddenly made no sense to me. When the hormones had cleared they'd left a hole. It was empty, and I couldn't stop myself from staring into it in confusion, rage, and sorrow. I called the clinic. I thought they would be used to dealing with the pain of suffocating regret.

"Morning is gone."

Silence.

"She doesn't work here anymore. Can I take a message?"

"Fuck you, baby killers!" I said before hanging up.

I'd made a mistake.

They just sucked it out.

She had said it like it was no big deal. Maybe not for Annie Money and many other women, but it was for me. What had I done?

I'd never thought about any of this before, and what it would mean to me, and how I would feel about any of it. They'd say, just cross that bridge when you come to it.

Just as I'd crossed over on that bridge, wondering if I should live or die?

For me a mistake as indelible as the black ink of the water below.

Yet Heraclitus says you can't stand in the same river twice.

But it didn't matter. The results were the same. And the power of what I'd done pulled me closer night by night to the black water. One day the pain became so unbearable I called a phone number a woman in the waiting room had folded into my hand. "In case you need to talk after it's, you know, over."

I unfolded the piece of pink paper with the drawing of a flower.

"Sad? Confused? You know we understand."

I liked the words "you know," as if we were in on something that would be okay as soon as I made the call. A tiny translucent female voice lilted up from the phone.

"Did he agree to marry you?"

"What?"

"He needs to marry you in Christ's eyes otherwise—"

"You're a fucking moron. A fucking freak."

Nailed with agony, I quickly hung up the phone.

And thus began my initiation. That summer I walked the streets where nobody knew me, stopped me, or asked, trying to figure out how this happened, praying the sheer force of my will would bring back the baby. I could not look at the people who passed me on the street. Their faces cultivated within me an exquisite despair. I could focus only on the rib of one sidewalk as it followed another.

Then one day, the edge of the sunlight caught me. The white points twitched on a dark patch of grass. For a second I became absorbed by that dark joy. Then the white pointed limbs moved. It made me want to cry, and I wished I'd never seen it.

OVER THE YEARS, I would ask McGilvery for reference after reference.

I made no enquiries into his life, and he made none into mine. Just the requests one would expect between a student and her academic advisor.

If I turned it over in my mind enough, the baby would come back again to breathe and pulse inside me. Take God's hand, and together we would enter the Kingdom of Ends.

But that is not evidential, I reminded myself every year for twenty years, as I walked through that city and this city now as letter by reference letter turned and cut inside me. The pregnancy had been far enough along that they'd told me the child was a boy. At least I thought they would say that; although, I never asked them. I didn't want to know. In the dream where the strange man comes and says you're the mother of my child I often thought about the boy who would have been my child. Sometimes I'd wonder if the child was very small, and had been taken away from me only to return at a later date. It was a different era. A private clinic. The stealing of a baby or foetus was rarely documented, only under the strangest circumstances. But in most cases that's just an urban myth. I knew that could never really happen.

I HAD A DREAM that night that I was in a cage. Burning through the bars, pitching back and forth, ratcheting over those tracks, staring through the bars as the black light glinted beyond me. It was a prison. Maybe a train. I was rocking and moving while I stared through the bars of a train car. Where was I? En route to where? I searched for the street names as the lights of the night flashed.

A bang on the door with a fist.

"Del! Del!" A familiar female voice scratched out from the other side. I looked up at the door of my apartment. Keys flashed. Jangled. Eyes. Arms held me until I slid to the side, crashing to the floor. I was lying on my stomach, my fingers twisting the ears of that orange sleeping bag.

The kid crouched in front of me. Cody or whatever his real name was. The black shards of hair. His eyes looked fast to the door then back at me. A shopping cart sat budged up against the door.

I clambered up. "What are you doing here?"

He raised his finger to his lips. Nodded to the door. Eyes squeezed dark and tight as a voice scratched from the other side. I kicked the cart out of the way.

"Let me in. Open up the door, Del. Open it up now."

The kid watched me as I edged to the door. Looked through the peephole. Krevice shrunk. Wavered through the tiny lens in that yellow light.

"We need to talk."

My mind flashed back and forth, wondering how I got home.

"It's late. You've made a hell of a racket. People are complaining."

I shouted back, "I'll call you tomorrow."

"Is someone in there? Somebody saw a male stranger in the building with a shopping cart. You can't bring those in here. It's against the law. They belong to the store."

His mouth crooked. His eyes squeezed tight on me again. Then she said, "Del, this is it. I'll be waiting for your call." Her feet pattered away.

Without moving my eyes from him, I felt my way across the room, my fingers twisted on the lamp. The light made that flash in his eyes die away. The rain had plastered down his hair, those black triangles, sharper than ever. Wet frenzied fur caught and bloody in the trap.

I retraced the evening's events. Forest. Bones. Sleeping bag. Black with rain and dirt. How did I get here? A sickening weight sagged inside me.

"What the fuck?" I said.

"I know," he said. "What's that bitch's problem?"

"How the fuck did all this happen?" I was circling the room with my arm. "You and me. This. Everything."

"Maybe you want to say thank you so fucking much." He gestured at the cart. "How the fuck did you get me here and save me from the wild animals and shit!"

He stood two inches away. I looked up. The rain darkening him. His eyes. His mouth. He held out his arms as if he was going to catch me and pull me in against my will. Look away. Look away. His staring eyes behind those sharp triangles were separating me away from myself again. If I could just move the hair out of his eyes, it would be okay. Just as I could still feel his body sliding along mine from before. I had wanted to find him. To straighten things out. To make clear that what happened didn't happen. But now that crust of a hard edge threatened to break apart. What was wrong with me? This was insane. I was insane. He was a kid, a street kid, and I was going to fuck him all over again. He couldn't be here. A mistake. I'd made a mistake, and now he had to go back to the forest. I backed away.

"I just saved your life. You could've been eaten by a mountain lion, or a bear. You know you're bleeding, right?" He held out a shirt. Covered in my blood.

I grabbed it from his hand. He flinched.

"You have to go," I said.

His eyes broke. "What the fuck you on about? You said I could stay." He pointed to the couch. "You said it right there. That night."

"That night never happened."

I limped across the room, swung the door open. He reached over and slammed it. "You promised."

"I don't believe in promises."

"Do you really want me to go back there? Don't make me go back there."

"I told you before, there are people who can help you."

"People!" His eyes came alight as if struck with a match. "You said if I came back—"

"You can go to Covenant House."

"It's closed."

"Not my problem."

"You said I could come back here. You absolutely—"

"A misunderstanding. I'm sorry," I said.

He looked down at the couch again. "You promised me in the dark."

"Those weren't promises. I should know. I'm a philosopher. We are very exact about promises." My voice was shaking. I couldn't get it to stop.

He showed no sign of leaving.

"I'll call the police," I said.

He looked at me with shock, and his eyes darkened. "You promised that night between us," his voice quavering.

"Nothing happened between us."

He stood in front of me breathing, panting. The hoodie. The long coat. The strap of his leather belt kept swinging.

"I don't even know you."

"Motherfucker are you serious? You know me."

"You can't be here right now. Nobody can find you here."

"They're never going to find us. We're going to run away. I'm going to take you for dinner. You ever been to Taco Bills? They're open all night."

"I'm calling the cops. Right now. Is that what you want?"

"You told me you were afraid."

Did I say he could come back here? I couldn't remember. His bruised eyes. His mouth.

"You said we were friends."

"I'd never say that."

"Now you're going to say you never followed me to Lurch."

"I don't know what you're talking about."

"That's a good one. Are we rewriting history now? You came to me, motherfucker. Not the other way around."

His words flared hot inside me.

"Yeah, admit it. This is what you wanted. Standing outside Lurch all last year. Stalking me. Making me follow you to the university. And now here. You have me right where you want me."

He didn't move. He just stood there. The neighbours.

"Look." My throat had tightened. I could barely talk now. "She's been calling here. Go! You have to go now."

"Listen. You're worried about that bitch?"

I lowered my voice, "I just want to make the situation clear," I said, trying not to look at him. "I have a position."

"Fuck your position. What did I tell you? What about my dream?"

"How many times do I have to tell you? I don't believe in dreams."

"Don't tell me that my dreams don't matter" he said, shaking. "They got me all the way here. You know something happened. It happened."

The phone rang. His face clenched and he turned away.

I moved toward the phone.

"Where are you going? Sit the fuck down."

The phone continued to ring.

I stood still, I don't know for how long, then at last, I rushed to the phone.

He ran over, pushed me out of the way, kicked the phone across the room. The receiver disconnected. It began to bleat.

Footsteps thumped down the hall and someone banged on the door.

A voice I didn't recognize called out, "We're trying to sleep here."

The phone still bleated.

He yelled at the door, "Shut the fuck up. We're having relationship problems."

The word relationship blurred with a dark, hot confusion that turned the world in a direction I didn't understand, just like years ago when that sharp white light had entered and turned against every fibre and will and cell inside me until the blue bled out of the sky. Maybe this was all right in some world I didn't understand: the sharp white light or the patch on the grass or the crocuses that pushed out of the ground or even his hands, the ones he'd touched me with that night months ago, the one he'd tattooed with my name. I now looked at his hands, his wrists. The white, long fingers, but the tattoos had vanished. I grabbed his arm.

"Where are they?"

He yanked his arm back. "What?"

"Your tattoos?"

"I don't fucking know," he shrugged. "Washed off or faded or something."

"What do you mean?"

"What do you mean what do I mean? They were just ink."

"They weren't real?"

"Who gives a fuck, motherfucker! I'm real." He banged his chest with his fist. "Don't you believe me? I'm standing right here."

"You're a liar."

"I'm not a liar," he yelled. "You can't fake a dream. My heart is bleeding. It's bleeding right now on this floor. Now you're stepping on it. Give me a knife. Give me something sharp. I'll show you what I'm on about."

He lunged hard and fast against the wall, hitting it with the flat of his foot, his shot foot, and falling back down.

"What about your foot? Did you lie about that, too? I thought you got shot.

"I never got shot," he cried. "I rolled it." He pulled a skateboard out of the cart. "See this! I'm not lying. Don't you believe me?"

"I don't know what you're talking about. You are a liar. A fucking liar."

"I'm not going fucking anywhere until you admit you wanted this. Tell me I'm not lying. Say it!" he said over and over, lunging against the wall, hitting it with the heel of his foot and falling back to the floor, shaking harder now.

The floor and the room shivered around me so I could barely see.

The neighbours!

I screamed at him, "Don't make me yell at you. I'm not your mother."

He stopped, lungs pumping his chest up and down. Then focused his eyes on me as sharp as a blade.

"Who are you to fucking talk about her? You think you're so special. You're nothing. You're a piece of fucking shit. You're like a dog that thinks it's God."

He sat down on the edge of the couch. The phone still bleated. He watched it as a glint of wet flashed and caught in his eyes. He pushed it away with the heel of his hand. It melted something inside me, melted the last sharp, iced shard of all I had done. Melted my credentials, melted those tears. Every edge. Frozen years, the ice of this cold edge, this sharp edge of years, this shard of ice that had stabbed my brain, heart, and body. Melted.

His face turned away from mine as he softly rocked, his leg tapping soundlessly against nothing. Tears were streaming down his face. The moon. The rain. Glints of him shivered. I imagined him as a baby, tiny, perfect, staring and sucking on his tongue, then as a child, looking at the world with wildness and curiosity, then black and dirty under the gaping hole. How had he gotten there? I thought. What's wrong with people? With me? Why are we all so horrible? He was a beautiful creature and didn't deserve to be shunned. My God, how could anyone not have wanted you? You are perfect and complete as you are. I reached over to move the hair from his eyes.

He recoiled. "She does that," he hissed, making a face of disgust, and pushing himself back up from the couch, glaring at me, his jaw clenched, face red, as his bad foot slipped. He fell to the floor, cracking his head on the edge of the marble side table as the lamp toppled, crashed, and the light went out.

He sat up, held his head. "I'm tired." Then lay back down again. Made a chuffing sound. Blood oozed out from his head.

His eyes eased closed. Almost as though he were asleep. I watched him lying there on my living room floor as the moon crested above my windowsill, glinting across the small puddle of blood that began to grow from the hole in his head.

Maybe I did promise.

Maybe.

In the dark.

I looked down at my hands. The moon didn't cast enough light for me to see as he lay on his back here next to me, bleeding to sleep on my floor.

"Wake up," I said, shaking him softly.

This was a dream. I just wanted to wake him up from this terrible dream. "Wake up from your dream," I said. But still he didn't move.

He was breathing hard, shallow breaths.

HE IS ASLEEP. He'll wake up soon.

Then under my fingers, he shakes. The blood seeps out no matter how hard I clench against the hole in his head. His breath, at first hoarse, grows smaller, slipping away with the moon shrinking out my window.

I reach out to the phone to call 911. Just as I pick up, I hear her voice,

"Let me talk to him."

My fingers stick together.

"Don't hang up," she begs up at me from my floor. Then sharply, "I want to talk to him. I want to talk to Cody."

"He's not here."

"Please, don't do that." Her voice catches. "Just listen to me. Please. Send my son home. I've called the cops. They're coming for you."

"Your son?"

"He's just a child."

"You're his mother?"

"Who the hell did you think I was?"

The phone slips from my hands.

The puddle around his head grows, glinting with even less of the moon now, and spreading across the tiles. The phone slides out of my hand just as I tell her, "Don't worry, it's going to be okay."

Outside, a car alarm goes off.

I call 911. "There's been an accident."

I lift one of his eyelids. The black pushes out the white and the iris, so the little lens can no longer shrink or grow with the light.

My hands clench tight together with the moon caught between.

Both hands touch my cheeks, tears, blood. The falling moon glints across this dark pool all around me.

I can't detect the breath through his nose.

The hair will no longer grow. The nails will, but only for a stint.

As has each tiny broken clock.

No matter how hard you try to turn them back.

Across this pool the moon grows dimmer as it falls farther away.

Your face alight with the last of this moon.

Wake up. Please wake up.

Don't worry. I won't let go.

Look at that! The last sliver of the moon rounds past my window.

Just like that star from your dream.

The siren in the distance turns, closer and closer with each wail.

And just then, as I cradle you, a tiny surge paddles up inside me.

Acknowledgements

Brian Kaufman for his incredible support, skill and belief in my work as well as all the great work of Karen Green and Cara Lang at Anvil Press;

Dr. Lisa Shapiro, my good friend, for reading multiple drafts and for her wisdom, generosity, and brilliance;

Dr. Liane Gabora, Zsuzsi Gartner, Christine Pountney, Michael Redhill, Martha Sharpe, Dr. Ori Simchen, and my agents Anna Archer and Sam Hiyate;

my students and colleagues at the University of British Columbia's Creative Writing Program;

my friends and family for being there for me all these years, my mother and father, my brothers, my grandmother, and especially Izzy and Mina;

Robert Kroestch who first encouraged me to write;

John Edward Sorrell, writer, teacher, friend;

A section of *Black Star*, under the title of "Bad Boy", appeared in the anthology, *Naked in Academe: Celebrating 50 Years of Creative Writing at UBC*, edited by Rhea Tregebov (McClelland & Stewart/Random House of Canada, 2014).

I would also like to thank the Canada Council and the BC Arts Council for their financial assistance during the writing of this book.

About the Author

MAUREEN MEDVED is a novelist, screenwriter, and playwright as well as an Associate Professor in the Creative Writing Program at the University of British Columbia. Her debut novel, *The Tracey Fragments*, was published by House of Anansi Press, and Maureen's screen adaptation—directed by Bruce MacDonald and starring Ellen Page—opened the Panorama program of the 57th annual Berlin International Film Festival and won the Manfred Salzgeber Prize. In 2009, Medved received the Artistic Achievement Award from Women in Film and Television, Vancouver. Maureen's plays have been produced across the country and her writing has been published in numerous literary journals and magazines. A collection of essays is forthcoming in 2019 (Anvil), and she is currently at work on a new novel. Medved lives in Vancouver.